Yearning for

the

Matchmaker

Book Six

Small Town

Matchmaker

Cheryl Wright

Copyright

Yearning for the Matchmaker
(Book Six, Small Town Matchmaker)

Copyright 2023 by Cheryl Wright

Small Town Romance Publications

Dedication

To Margaret Tanner, my very dear friend and fellow author, for her enduring encouragement and friendship.

To Alan, my husband of over forty-eight years, who has been a relentless supporter of my writing and dreams for many years.

To You, my wonderful readers, who encourage me to continue writing these stories. It is such a joy knowing so many of you enjoy reading my stories as much as I love writing them for you.

Table of Contents

Chapter One

Crystal Springs – 1880s

It was still early, and the store was quiet. Dennis Andrews, the mercantile store owner, hadn't even opened the doors it was so early.

Boxes were piling up in the storeroom, and Dennis knew he needed to put everything in its place. He ran his store like a well-oiled clock, and that was because he was meticulous.

He drank down the last of the bitter coffee and washed his mug, then left it to dry on the rack. Now he was ready to work.

Dennis pulled on his brown vest—the one he always wore in the store over a crisp white shirt, then tied his half apron around his waist. Appearances were everything.

As he headed into the store from his residence, a tap on the door of the store caught his attention. He hurried to see who was so impatient for the store to be opened. The plain gray jacket caught his eye, and he had no doubt it was Ethel Bowman, the school Marm.

He hurried to unlock the door. "Good morning, Miss Bowman," he said pleasantly, although he wasn't feeling happy about his routine being disturbed. "How may I help you on this sunny day?"

The school teacher stared at him. "The sun is barely up!" she exclaimed, then suddenly clamped her mouth shut. "Oh my goodness. It really is early, isn't it?"

Dennis refrained from agreeing with her, and merely raised an eyebrow instead. "I am an early riser," he told her instead. "This time of day, I normally restock the shelves. What can I do for you, Miss Bowman?"

She waved a gloved hand in front of herself. "Ethel, please. I get enough *Miss Bowman* from my students." She seemed to ponder his question for a moment, then suddenly studied Dennis. "How would you feel if I brought my students to the store for a lesson?"

"All of them? At once?" Dennis asked. His heart thudded. Twelve children running through his store all at once, creating havoc with his well-ordered shelves? What sort of mess would he be left with? He wasn't sure how to answer. The last thing he wanted was to lose business from the townspeople if he refused, but he had to think of the consequences of such an event.

"Oh goodness, no," Ethel told him. "That would be asking for trouble. No, the younger children will be cared for at the schoolhouse, and I will accompany the older students here. It would be a lesson in arithmetic."

Dennis felt immediate relief. "How would that work?" he asked. It was all in the details, especially when children were involved. Most of the parents were unable to control their offspring while shopping, so he needed to know how Ethel Bowman planned on keeping her older students under control.

"Each student will have two dollars to spend, and no more. They will choose items that fit within that monetary range." She stood at the counter and glanced about. "Before I breach the idea with my students, I need assurance from you. Can you cope with this lesson in your store?"

Cope? Dennis Andrews could deal with anything, and most people in town knew it. "Of course," he said firmly. "When did you plan on having this lesson at the store?"

"Tomorrow afternoon," she said, studying him. "The parents were advised some time ago, but the students are currently unaware of this extra-curricular activity I have planned."

Since the parents already knew, there was no way out. Not that it mattered—each child would spend money in his store. How could Dennis deny paying customers? "What time should I expect them to arrive?" It was a crucial piece of information he needed to know. There was nothing like being prepared.

Ethel smiled. Dennis couldn't recall seeing her smile before—it completely transformed her face. And it made his heart skip a beat.

What utter nonsense! Why he would feel that way seeing a woman smile, he had no idea. And it wasn't as though he really knew her, as they'd barely spoken two sentences to each other before today.

"Around three. At least that's the plan. Thank you, Dennis. I shall see you then."

Ethel Bowman was gone as quickly as she'd arrived, which meant Dennis could get back to his routine.

There were fewer boxes cluttering the storeroom now than there had been two hours earlier. It could have been even less if he'd had someone behind the counter. Dennis rarely thought about marrying, but it was times like this he did.

Each time he'd fallen into a rhythm, the bell over the door beckoned him out. It was frustrating, but there was little he could do about it. Short of marrying that was. So far, no one had caught his eye, and therefore he was still single.

Dennis knew he would be fussy about a wife. It would have to be someone who thought in a similar fashion to him. She would be meticulous about neatness, and would have to be an excellent cook. Not that he would admit it to anyone else, but Dennis lived on canned food from his store, as well as sausages and bacon. He occasionally ate at the diner, but mostly at home.

Joel Evans had all but banned him from the bakery—Dennis couldn't even remember what that was over. Most likely it was his own fault. He was fully aware he could be unpleasant at times. He needed to work on that.

Anyway, Joel now had a new girl working there, what was her name? It might mean he could visit the bakery without Joel's interference. Who knew what delicious pastries they had there now?

Dennis sighed. He would probably give the bakery a wide berth. He didn't need trouble. He brought enough of that on himself already. The bell over the door tinkled again. If it wasn't for the fact it alerted him to buying customers, Dennis would dismantle that bell and throw it in the trash.

By the time he reached the counter, Allie Hubertson was standing there. "Good morning, Allie," he said cheerfully, despite the headache he was developing. "How may I help you?"

Allie smiled, and it lit up her face. She'd worked at the diner for a long time now, but Dennis still didn't know her well. "Do you know when our regular order is arriving?" she asked.

"Let me check," he said, then pulled out a list from under the counter and flicked through the pages. "It should be tomorrow or Friday."

Allie sighed. "I was afraid you were going to say that. In that case, I need some supplies to tide us over."

Dennis reached for a box and joined Allie on the other side of the counter. "Let me see that list," he said, then began to fill the order.

"What's on the menu this evening?" Dennis asked cordially as he helped Allie find her supplies.

She turned and faced him, one eyebrow raised. "We don't see you there often. Feeling a bit hungry today?" She laughed then, and the sound sent shock waves through him. "I'm making chicken pot pie for the special. There will also be steak and veg. Apple pie for dessert, plus the usual cakes and muffins."

Dennis could almost taste it. Why he didn't dine there more often, he didn't know. More than likely it was the cost, although in the scheme of things, it wasn't expensive.

"Should I save a table for you?" Allie asked. "Not that we often fill up, but I can give you the best table in the diner if I know in advance."

Dennis was sorely tempted, especially if it meant Allie would be looking. after him. He suddenly halted. What was wrong with him today? First it was Ethel Bowman, then Allie. His mind was playing tricks on him. Dennis was not interested— no matter who it was, he did not want to marry. Just because he enjoyed matching other people didn't mean *he* needed a wife. He was blissfully happy with his life the way it was.

Well, perhaps not blissfully, but things were going well. Weren't they?

"Dennis? Are you alright?" Allie's hand went to his arm. "Should I get Marcus to come and check you out?"

Marcus? The doctor? He shook his head. "I'm fine. Sorry, I was just thinking, is all."

Allie nodded. A frown creased her pretty face. "As long as you're certain?" She didn't seem convinced.

She was sweet, worrying about him. Dennis never got sick, but today his mind was playing games with him. "I've been unpacking boxes all morning, and filling the storeroom."

"As well as serving customers. Dennis, you need help." Her words were firm, and he knew she was right.

Allie sounded more than a little concerned, which was thoughtful of her, but she barely knew him except to come in here and get supplies for the diner. "I do have help. You know that."

"Teenagers coming in after school a couple of days a week is not what I meant. You need a wife." Allie stood with her hands on her hips. "Someone who will be here all day, and give you a break."

If he hadn't been so shocked at her words, Dennis would have laughed. "Are you applying for the position?" he asked, then chuckled.

Allie turned beet red. "I…no. I have enough to do running the diner." She harrumphed then. "I'll be back later for my supplies." She turned to leave, but Dennis stopped her.

"It was a joke, Allie. I have no intention of getting married. But I might have to employ someone to help me. It is getting a bit too much these days."

Allie stared at him. "The older we get, the harder it gets. At least that's what everyone tells me," she said.

She smiled and he knew she was joking. It made Dennis smile too. "I'll have to think seriously about employing someone. Even part-time would be a help. I don't suppose you know anyone?" He didn't want to employ a stranger, although it might come to that.

Perhaps Ethel Bowman might recommend one of her older students? Or perhaps not. He'd heard she was a stickler for them doing homework. Besides, it was during the day he needed the most assistance. Dennis sighed. He really did need help.

Allie shook her head. "Sorry, I can't think of anyone right now. But I'll let you know if I do." She glanced down at the list again. "I think that's everything I need for now," Allie said, bringing him out of his thoughts again.

They headed to the front of the store and the counter, where Dennis added the purchases to the diner's account book. "Let me carry them to the diner for you," he offered. The box was not overly large, but it was heavy. "I can close the store for a few minutes."

Allie accepted his offer, and Dennis turned the 'Back in Five Minutes' sign around. The fresh air would do him good.

Allie led Dennis into the diner's kitchen, and indicated for him to leave the supplies on the counter. "Thank you, Dennis," she said. "I appreciate it."

Dennis was certain she did. He spun around and waved a hand in farewell. He didn't want to leave the mercantile closed any longer than necessary. Hurrying back to the store, he could see people already waiting outside the store. Of all the luck— on the one rare occasion he left, customers were queuing. He should have known. The store always had a constant stream of customers. It was one of the reasons he needed help.

Two strangers were waiting—an older man, and a woman who appeared to be in her late twenties. The man stood over her. They appeared to be arguing. She seemed very unhappy, agitated even.

Dennis noticed a wagon stood nearby. The closer he got to the store, the easier it became to hear their conversation. The woman was quite upset. "Please, Father," she seemed to almost beg.

Now only a couple of feet away, he could see she was crying. He didn't want to get in the middle of a family discussion, but he needed to open the store again. "Good morning," he said as pleasantly as possible under the circumstances, then stepped closer.

The moment he did, the man pulled a gun on him. Dennis's heart hammered. Until now, he'd never been robbed. Whatever they wanted, he would give them. It wasn't worth his life to withhold money nor product.

His hands now in the air, the man finally spoke. "Unlock the door, and do it quickly." He indicated for Dennis to turn around, then shoved a gun in his back the moment he did.

"Father, please don't," the woman pleaded with him.

"Shut yer stinkin' mouth!" he screamed at his daughter. "Just leave. I don't need you here."

"Alright, I will," she shouted, her voice wavering. Suddenly, Dennis heard her running along the boardwalk.

"Good riddance to bad rubbish," the man with the gun spat out. "Unlock the door," he said again. "And hurry up about it. Yer just wastin' my time."

Dennis couldn't believe it. He had little cash in the store—he banked his takings at the end of every day. Just as well, too. His hand shook as he tried to open the door. "Give me the key!" the man demanded. Dennis complied. Until now, he hadn't really seen the man's face. Now he was able to glance at him and take in a few of his features. The sheriff would want to know details when Dennis reported the robbery.

"Git inside," he was ordered, and again, Dennis did what he was told. It wasn't worth his life.

"Bart Dougherty," the sheriff barked. "Drop your gun and slowly turn around. Then put your hands in the air."

Dennis saw the shocked look on the other man's face. Then his face screwed up in anger. "That no-good cow—she did this. She's as bad as her mother was."

Another voice shouted this time. "Drop the gun and turn around slowly." Dennis recognized that voice too. It was former sheriff Wyatt Holt. His relief was palpable, knowing the two most capable men in Crystal Springs were there to arrest this horrid man.

The stranger leaned down and dropped the gun to the ground, anger still covering his face. "Now slowly remove the gun from your boot," Sheriff Tommy Garratt said, and watched closely as the second gun was extracted.

"I'll never forgive you for this, Rachel," the gunslinger screeched, despite his daughter being nowhere in sight. He then spat on the boardwalk. Dennis cringed. What a filthy beast the man was. Thank goodness for his daughter running to the sheriff. Where he would be now, Dennis didn't know, but was convinced he would probably be lying dead on the mercantile floor.

Chapter Two

Rachel Dougherty sat in the sheriff's office sipping a glass of water. Her eyes were filled with tears, but she'd learned not to let them flow. Doing so earned her a hard slap to the face from her father.

How that awful man could be her father, Rachel had no idea. He was the total opposite of her mother, who was the most placid person she'd ever known. They'd lost her many years ago, and although devastated at her passing by her father's hand, Rachel was content she was at rest and away from the continuous aggression they lived in.

"Miss Dougherty? Are you alright?" A stranger's voice cut into her thoughts, and Rachel stared at him. She didn't know the man and cringed. Was he going to hurt her?

"This is Doctor Marcus Ryan," the sheriff said gently. "He will check you over."

Rachel nodded. She hadn't even heard him come in. "Is…is the store owner alright?" This time, she couldn't fight back her tears. "Please, tell me," she begged. "My father didn't kill him, did he?" She placed her hands on her face and sobbed.

"It's shock," Marcus said, as he put a hand to her back.

"My father?" Rachel asked when she finally quelled the sobbing. "I hope he rots in hell." She stared at the sheriff as she spoke the words, and saw his shocked expression.

"Why is that, Miss Dougherty?" He glanced across at the doctor, but Doctor Ryan gave nothing away.

She swallowed hard. "He killed my mother. Hit her one too many times. He's an evil man, and I hate him." Tears ran down her face again, and Rachel wanted her nightmare to finally come to an end.

The town rallied around her, and Rachel was grateful. She sat in the parlor of the preacher and his wife, and felt truly wanted for the first time in her life.

"How are you feeling, Rachel?" Faith asked gently.

Rachel glanced up at her. Until now, she'd kept her gaze on her hands intertwined on her lap. "I think I'm still in shock," she finally answered. "That he's finally been caught. The man is pure evil. My mother and I tried to get away from him for many years."

Faith glanced across at her husband, Preacher Clyde Walters. "You're safe now," the preacher said quietly, as if trying to reassure her. "You are among friends here in Crystal Springs."

Rachel hoped he was right, but how would the townsfolk forgive her for simply being with her father when he intended to rob the store?

"If you hadn't gone for the sheriff, who knows if Dennis would be alive now." Faith reached across and touched her arm. "You probably saved his life." She smiled tentatively, and Rachel appreciated the gesture.

"He wouldn't. Be alive, that is. Father would have killed him the moment he emptied the cash box. That's the way he works."

Faith stood and came to sit on the arm of Rachel's chair. "He won't be doing that ever again," Faith assured her. "You are now safe from his violent behavior. The townsfolk here will be thankful to you for saving our Dennis."

Rachel sniffled. Tears were forming in her eyes again, and her heart felt as though it was throbbing. She didn't feel like she'd done a good deed, but everyone she'd come in contact with so far had told her she did.

"He told me I'm..." Rachel closed her eyes and tears ran down her cheeks. When she opened them, two pairs of eyes were watching her. "He said I'm evil. Spawned of the devil himself." She broke down again, but felt a comforting hand on her shoulder. Rachel glanced up. "I'm sorry," she whispered. "You don't need the likes of me in your home."

Faith and Clyde glanced at each other. Briefly, but it was enough Rachel noticed.

The preacher spoke up then. "You are exactly where you need to be," he said firmly. "I don't believe you have even a grain of evil in you."

Rachel's heart rate subsided. She hoped the preacher was right.

Clyde walked across the room and reached for her hands. "Lord," he said quietly as he stood in front of her, his eyes closed. "I ask that you watch over this young woman who has been abused and violated by her father. Keep her safe from harm, and ease the pain in her heart." He gently squeezed her hands and Rachel felt hot tears run down her cheeks yet again. She was certain by now she had shed all the tears there were to shed. "Amen," the preacher said.

"Amen," Faith said too.

"Thank you," Rachel said, her voice breaking. What she would do now, she had no idea.

"I think a nice pot of tea is in order," Faith said, then left the room before Rachel had an opportunity to refuse. These were nice people. Good people. Not that she'd expected anything different from a preacher and his wife. They'd offered to take her in, no questions asked. Although soon after the incident with her father, Rachel was certain it would be all over town. By now, everyone would have heard the news. They would know there was a killer in town, and she was his daughter.

"You are safe here," Clyde said gently. "No one blames you for what happened."

If only she could believe his words. "Thank you for the reassurance, but I'm sure Mr. Andrews wouldn't agree." She bit her lip then. Her pain ran deep. "My father has killed dozens of men over the years. Since he murdered Mother, he's used me as bait—to make his victims feel at ease." Would the pain of her mother's murder never leave her?

Rachel tightly closed her eyes.

She heard a gasp and opened her eyes again. Faith sat herself back on the arm of the chair. "I'm so sorry you had to endure all that," she said in a whisper. "We are always here if you want to talk."

Rachel nodded. She was bereft of words. The kindness of the townsfolk in Crystal Springs was difficult to understand. And yet, here she was, being enveloped in kindness by complete strangers.

Then a thought hit her. "I...I want to apologize to Dennis Andrews. My presence made him feel comfortable to approach my father. He could have been killed."

Faith pulled her into an embrace. She hadn't felt arms around her in a very long time—since she'd lost her mother to her murdering father. Rachel melted into Faith's arms, and stayed for what seemed a very long time. "Thank you," she whispered as she straightened up. "I needed that."

She glanced up at Faith, and the other woman smiled tentatively. They both knew that hug would not fix what was broken inside her, but it was a good start.

Chapter Three

Dennis lay in bed far longer than usual. He'd literally dodged a bullet yesterday, and now he was less than eager to open the store today. Except he knew he must.

Apart from anything else, Ethel Bowman was bringing her students to the store. Perhaps he could get one of the teenagers in to assist him? It had been on his mind yesterday. Then his world tilted. And not for the better.

He sat on the side of the bed and shook his head, trying to clear away the cobwebs. Marcus had told Dennis he was in shock, and it could last for several days, even longer. He brushed it aside. Now he wasn't so sure he should.

How long had he sat there simply thinking? Far too long, he decided. He went straight to the bathroom and freshened up, then dressed. Today was no different to any other day—he had work to do. In fact, today would likely be busier than his average workday due to the students coming by.

He'd only moments ago finished his coffee when he heard knocking on the door. Not today, please, he silently begged, but the banging continued. Yesterday he would have almost run to see who was there. Today his steps were slow. Dennis felt as though he was most at a standstill.

When he lifted the blind on the window, he saw it was Ethel. An enormous sigh of relief left him, and it surprised Dennis. When had he become so fearful? Of course, he knew the answer—being held at gunpoint by a crazed and violent gunslinger was the reason. Reaching to unlock the door, his hands shook. He glanced at them in shock. He'd vowed not to let yesterday's events affect him, and yet, the proof was right in front of him.

He was finally able to unlock the door and invited Ethel inside. "Good morning," Dennis said, not as enthusiastic as he would normally be with a customer.

"Oh, Dennis," Ethel said, then pulled him into a tight hug. "I am so glad to see you in one piece. It must have been a dreadful experience." When she pulled back, he saw the distress on her face. "We should cancel the student's visit today."

"There is no need to change your plans," Dennis told her. "I will secure help. What time this afternoon works for you? I'm sorry—I don't recall."

"If you're certain? You've had a traumatic experience."

Ethel was correct. It had been traumatic, but he'd prefer to put it all behind him. "You set a time, and I will ensure the store is ready." He forced himself to smile. It was the last thing he wanted, but keeping busy was likely the best thing he could do.

"Shall we make it three o'clock?"

"I look forward to it," Dennis said.

Ethel nodded, although she still didn't seem convinced. She squeezed his hand, then quickly left him alone.

After the morning rush, he would close the store while he rustled up some help for this afternoon. Keeping busy was definitely what he needed to do.

He locked the door, then headed for the storeroom. There was plenty to do to make up for yesterday's lost time.

When there was banging at the door again, Dennis checked his pocket watch. He found it difficult to believe he'd already been working for close to an hour. He'd even missed the store's opening time. That wasn't like him at all.

The closer he got to the door, the clearer it became who was standing there. Rachel Dougherty. His steps halted. Dennis wasn't certain he wanted to speak with her. Or even be in the same room with her. How dangerous was the gunslinger's daughter?

He glanced at her through the window. She looked tense, which wasn't surprising. After all, she'd been part of the ruse to make him feel comfortable opening up the store. Until her father pulled a gun on him. Then rammed it into his back.

Dennis shuddered. Would he never get the memory out of his mind?

Hand shaking, he reached for the lock. He had never been a nervous man. Now he was reduced to a frightened wreck. Dennis took a long and fortifying breath. He would not let that one incident rule his life.

Forcing himself to smile for the second time today, he unlocked the door and pulled it wide open. "Good morning," he said, far more cheerfully than he felt. "Apologies for the locked door. I lost track of time," he told his unwanted visitor. Once she was inside, he closed the door and went behind the counter. He needed to keep his day as close to normality as possible.

"Good morning," Rachel Dougherty said, her smile pensive. "I…" She took a deep breath then, and let it out in a whoosh. "I came to apologize. My father forced me to…"

Dennis put a hand up to stop her words. "No need to apologize. Without you, I'm certain I would not be here today. I should be thanking you."

She pursed her lips. Did that mean she didn't believe him? The sheriff had explained everything. Rachel was an innocent victim in all this. She'd been coerced with violence and finally put an end to her father's evil ways. "I'm sure it has been traumatic for you, as it has…" He suddenly stopped speaking. Did he really want to admit to this stranger how traumatized he'd been left by her father's actions?

She glanced down at her hands. "I'm truly sorry," she said in a whisper. "How can I make it up to you?"

Shaking his head, Dennis knew it wasn't her fault. The sheriff would have locked her up at the same time he jailed her father if she was truly guilty of a crime. Besides, she saved his life, and that was no mean feat. Bart Dougherty was vicious, and if she hadn't gone for the sheriff, he would have killed both Dennis and his daughter without another thought. He was absolutely convinced of it.

"Please," she begged. "I need to make it up to you. There must be a way." She continued to twist her hands in front of herself, and it made Dennis realize she was genuinely upset.

"I need help in the store later today," he blurted out before he could stop himself. It was too late to take it back, so he might as well tell her the details. Then it was up to Rachel whether she accepted. "The town teacher, Ethel Bowman, is bringing her senior students here at three o'clock. They will purchase goods to the value of two dollars each." She stared at him. "It's an arithmetic lesson," he explained.

"I will gladly help," Rachel told him. "Since I'm already here, why don't you show me around the store and explain how you work?" She smiled then, and her face lit up. Dennis felt a flutter in his heart. He hoped he wasn't about to have a heart attack. "Are you alright?" Rachel asked, then touched his arm. The flutter of his heart got worse. Did he need to see the doc?

"I just need a moment," he said, his voice shaking. If he truly was having a heart attack, he wouldn't make it to the doctor's office alone. He backed himself onto the chair he kept behind the counter for quiet times, so he could rest. Not that he had many quiet times these days. The town was flourishing, and they had customers from the stagecoach as well. It was mostly busy at the store now, which is the reason he desperately needed help.

"I don't pay much," he blurted out. Why couldn't his brain and mouth cooperate with each other?

She beamed, and he was certain she was laughing at him. "I don't want to be paid," she told him. "I want to make up for yesterday's travesty." She reached up and brushed a stray piece of hair behind her ear. It took all his effort not to fix the hair on the other side of her face.

Perhaps he should see the doc after all. His heart and his mind were playing games with him.

Chapter Four

Rachel followed Dennis around the store as he explained where everything belonged. He showed her how to measure items like oats and flour, how to wrap soap, a bunch of flowers, even how to fold gowns. She seemed to pick things up quickly.

Lastly, nervously, he showed her where he kept the cash tin. It was locked and out of sight behind the counter. She understood his anxiety when it came to his money, and Rachel reached out and touched his arm. "I'm not interested in your money, Dennis," she whispered. "My being here is all about reparation."

"Reparation?" he asked. He appeared shocked.

"What my father did to you was appalling. I couldn't control him, but I can control how I mend fences."

Dennis seemed even more confused. "Mend fences?"

"Between you and me," Rachel said. "I do not know how long I'll stay in Crystal Springs. I have to stay for my father's trial, according to the sheriff. Apparently, I'm a witness, so I can't leave." She raised an eyebrow then, wondering what Dennis thought of her hanging around.

"Here comes a customer," Dennis told her. "You look after her and I'll step in if you need help. Alright?"

Rachel nodded as the customer approached the counter.

"Good morning, Allie," Dennis said with a smile on his face. "This is Rachel. She is going to help in the store today."

Allie looked Rachel up and down, then her jaw dropped. "Aren't you…"

Words seemed to fail her, and Rachel interrupted. "Yes, I'm his daughter. But I'm nothing like him. I promise."

"Rachel ran to the sheriff's office, Allie. If it wasn't for her, I wouldn't be here today."

The nod Allie gave was almost non-existent. "I came to see if my order came in. And to see if you were alright, Dennis. If you hadn't carried my supplies to the diner…" She was visibly upset, although none of it was her fault.

"It would have still happened," Dennis said quickly.

"If Dennis had been in the store when we arrived, he would be dead now. My father would have shot him in cold blood before even opening his mouth."

Rachel heard Dennis gasp. "He's done it before? Killed people, I mean?"

"Many, many times. Previously, I had no opportunity to stop him." She shuddered at the memory. "My father is the most evil person I have ever known." Her voice shook, and tears swam in her eyes. Rachel turned her back to the pair standing nearby.

She was startled by an arm going around her, then pulling her close. "Clearly, it's not your fault," Allie said gently. "You saved our Dennis's life. Thank you." She whispered the last words, and Rachel almost didn't hear them.

The bell over the door tinkled, and Rachel pulled out of Allie's grip. She swiped at her eyes, then stepped a little closer to Dennis. Allie understood and again went to the other side of the counter.

"To answer your question, Allie, I believe your order will arrive tomorrow. Do you need another top up?"

"Only a few things. I'll manage by myself." She said, then lifted her basket, presumably to show she didn't need a box.

"Do you mind if Rachel assists you? She's trying to learn the ropes." Dennis glanced toward her, and Rachel fought the urge to flinch. He was right, though. She needed to learn.

"Shall we?" Allie said as cheerfully as she seemed to be able to muster. Rachel felt she still wasn't happy about her helping in the store.

"I promise," she said in a whisper when they were away from the counter and out of earshot of Dennis. "I mean no harm. I want to repair the damage my father did. Perhaps we can be friends?"

Allie turned to stare at her. "Friends? That will remain to be seen. My concern is with Dennis's welfare. Nothing else."

Rachel nodded. She completely understood and even admired the way the townsfolk rallied around their own. "What may I do to help you?" she asked.

Allie handed her the short list, and Rachel was pleased she remembered where most of the items were stocked. "I also need some lemons," Allie said when they were back at the counter. "Please put everything on the diner's account."

Dennis stood watching over her shoulder as she entered the details. "Would you like me to carry your shopping back to the diner for you?" Dennis asked when Rachel finished.

"There's no weight in this. I'll be fine, thank you, Dennis." Allie turned and left the store.

Moments later, another customer, Mrs. Hargreaves, Dennis told her, came to the front counter. She looked Rachel up and down, then sniffed. "Good morning, Dennis," she said, then turned to Rachel. "Who are you?"

"I'm Rachel," she said, purposely leaving out her surname for fear of repercussions. "I'm helping Dennis in the store today."

Mrs. Hargreaves placed her purchases on the counter. "Please put them on my account." She watched Rachel's every move, ensuring she wasn't overcharged. Dennis studied her and made sure no mistakes were made. Did that mean Mrs. Hargreaves was a difficult customer? Rachel surmised that was the case.

She placed all the woman's purchases in a paper bag and handed them over. "Thank you for your business, Mrs. Hargreaves."

The other woman seemed shocked at her words, but smiled. "Thank you, too. Good day to you both," she said, then left the store.

Dennis turned to her. "You seem to have the hang of it. This afternoon will be the test."

Rachel swallowed. She only hoped she could cope with the sudden bedlam Dennis expected. "How many children should we expect?" she asked, trying not to sound terrified.

Dennis scratched his head. "That's a good question, and one I didn't think to ask. I'd guess only six or eight at most. It's only the seniors who are coming."

Rachel nodded—that should be quite manageable for both of them. At least, she hoped it was. Dennis would have managed without her, but since the timing was right, Rachel could at least take some of the pressure off him. Even if that was only through packing their purchases and saving Dennis the effort.

With the store now empty, Rachel took a moment to relax. The mercantile certainly was busy. It made her wonder how Dennis managed on a day-to-day basis. "Can I get you a coffee?" Rachel asked after a couple of minutes. "You might as well benefit from the lull in customers."

A smile crossed Dennis's face. "That would be nice. The kitchen is through there," he said, pointing. "I have mine black and no sugar."

Rachel headed toward the kitchen. Today had been nice. She still had several hours before she finished for the day. It wasn't what she'd expected from her day, but she felt overwhelmingly happy being able to make the day easier for Dennis.

Not that it would ever make up for what her father put the store owner through.

Crystal Springs was a lovely town. It was a pity she would have to move on. With no paying jobs available in town, she had no way to support herself. Besides, she was already facing the prejudice from several townsfolk. Rachel didn't want to live like that. She'd rather move on and have no one know her history. It was hard enough being the unknown element in a new town, but being known as a killer's daughter? That was a completely different situation altogether.

Chapter Five

The coffee Rachel had made for him earlier was actually drinkable. Dennis's own coffee was like dishwater. And now she'd served up a light lunch for him, using ingredients from the mercantile. She was handy to have around.

He was already seeing the value of having someone like Rachel working for him regularly. Dennis wanted to see how she handled the seniors from the school this afternoon. Then, if she managed, he may ask her to come back tomorrow.

After that—he would have to see. It wasn't like he couldn't afford to pay her, because he could. He earned a nice profit from the mercantile. In fact, his profits were sitting in the bank growing by the day. Since he spent all his days in the store, he had nothing to spend his money on. He rarely went anywhere except to church, and he lived behind the store. He'd paid off his mortgage quickly.

When he moved to Crystal Springs, little did he know what a goldmine the store would be. Providing high-quality goods for sale at a reasonable price was the key. He was certain of that. But now he needed to look after himself. Was it really only yesterday he'd been told he needed a wife?

With everything that had happened, it seemed farther back than that. Not that it was new. Townsfolk had been telling him for years he needed to marry. Only Dennis wasn't interested—he enjoyed being a bachelor. He preferred being his own boss and making his own decisions.

The bell over the door tinkled, and he stood. "Stay there and enjoy your meal," Rachel told him. At first he hesitated, but Rachel was gone in a matter of moments. He could certainly get used to this.

He heard muffled voices coming from the store, and a short time later, the bell tinkled again. It wasn't long after that Rachel returned.

"That was Allie again," she said. "She forgot to purchase blueberries. I added them to her account." Rachel smiled and his heart fluttered in the same way it had earlier. Dennis wasn't sure what to make of it. "I'm really enjoying helping you out today," Rachel added with a meek smile.

"Wait until this afternoon's school visit is over before you make that decision," Dennis told her with a grin. "To be honest, I can already see it will be far easier with you here to help."

Rachel glanced up at him and smiled. "I'm looking forward to it. No doubt it will be interesting." She picked up her soiled plate and carried it to the sink, then turned back to check Dennis's coffee. It was almost empty, and she refilled it without asking.

"Thank you," Dennis told her. "Today has been interesting."

Rachel tilted her head to the side. "You haven't had help in the store before?" Her frown marred her face, and it made Dennis frown too.

"No. Yes. I mean, I have, but only teenagers from town. They're very irresponsible and are only interested in being paid." He drank down almost half his coffee. "I can barely get them to sweep the boardwalk, let alone stack the shelves."

"That's awful," Rachel said, then washed their dishes. "Have you had enough to eat?"

"I have, thank you. I often skip lunch, so this was nice."

She turned to face him. "You skip meals? You shouldn't do that." Rachel stopped talking abruptly then. "I didn't mean…" Her words trailed off, and she suddenly looked terrified.

Dennis shoved his chair back and went to her, then stepped back as she cringed against the counter. "Rachel," he said gently. "I will never harm you. I apologize if I scared you."

She shuddered and slowly straightened. "I…I know," she whispered. "Old habits die slowly. I'll be fine. I just need to be alone."

Dennis nodded and left her alone as she'd asked. It finally became clear to him what she'd been dealing with all her life. He couldn't wait for the court case against Bart Dougherty. The man deserved the noose.

Three o'clock came around slowly. Rachel seemed to shrink to a shell of her former self. Until the students arrived, right on time. They spread out through the store and took their time deciding on their purchases.

Their teacher, Ethel Bowman, was there, overseeing both their behavior and their purchasing. Several pupils were fairly quick with their buying, but others took their time. Rachel was a godsend. Having her there meant they could both serve customers at the same time.

While Rachel tended to the regular customers, Dennis looked after their more rowdy shoppers. Not that he'd had a lot of time to notice, but most of the townsfolk had taken to Rachel. She wasn't convinced that would transpire after what happened.

"Are you coping alright?" Dennis asked during a lull in the frenzied buying. She certainly seemed calm enough.

"I am. People here are...lovely." Rachel raised an eyebrow then, as if to portray how surprising it was to her. "You have a wonderful store, too. One of the best I've seen, if not the best."

Dennis almost puffed out his chest with pride, but was interrupted by Harry Jones with his purchases. Ethel stood two steps behind the young man, checking his mathematical skills. With Ethel nearby, Dennis almost felt he was the one being tested.

He mentally added up the boy's combined purchases—they came five cents under the maximum amount allowed. He bagged the boy's purchases and handed him the change.

"Well done, Harry. You can go outside and wait with the others," Ethel told him. The boy did as he was told.

Dennis glanced through the glass window of the door. They were about halfway through this exercise. "The students have done well so far," he told the schoolteacher.

"They have, but these students are slower than the rest. I'd hoped to be out of your hair before this." The dismay on Ethel's face bothered Dennis.

"It really is fine. Rachel offered to help for the day, and it's worked out wonderfully." The bell over the door tinkled as another customer came inside. Dennis glanced across to see Rachel dealing with another local, again taking the load off him. She really was worth her weight in gold.

Dennis rubbed a hand across his chin. Maybe Allie was right—he needed more permanent help in the store. But was Rachel the right person for the job? Was she even staying in town beyond the court case? The last thing he wanted to do was train her in all aspects of the day-to-day running of the store, then have her leave.

He studied her as she served two more customers she'd isolated from the school students. He appreciated she'd done that. It helped keep his customers happy.

"That's it," Ethel finally said. "All my pupils are outside. Thank you, Dennis, for agreeing to help with this exercise."

He grinned then. "It wasn't all one-sided. They made purchases, remember?"

Ethel laughed, thanked him again, then left, taking her students back to the schoolhouse.

"Phew, that was hectic," Rachel said when the store was again empty and quiet. She leaned back and smiled. "But it was good. Your store gets quite busy. I really don't know how you manage alone."

Before he had a chance to answer, she'd hurried off and straightened the shelves and refilled those that needed it.

Dennis stood back and smiled. Today had been one of his most delightful days for a very long time.

Chapter Six

Rachel hurried out to the storeroom. She'd mentally assessed what items she needed to refill on the shelves. But now she was unsure if she'd recalled correctly.

Heavy footsteps alerted her that Dennis was heading her way. "Can I help?" he asked as she glanced about the large room.

Feeling defeated, she confessed. "I can't remember what is needed," she answered, knowing she'd let him down.

"Did you write a list?"

At first, Rachel thought he was joking, but Dennis appeared to be serious. She shook her head.

"I always write a list," he told her. "There's usually far too much to remember. Here," he said, handing her a notepad and pencil. "Take this one. I can get another." He left the storeroom then, and Rachel followed.

They moved around the store stealthily, going from shelf to shelf. It was easier with Dennis next to her.

He knew where everything belonged. "Two cakes of lavender soap," he said, and Rachel wrote it down. "Three jars of bath salts, and a face cloth." They continued compiling a list, shelf by shelf. This was far easier than her original method.

She glanced up at Dennis. He appeared much more relaxed than he was this morning. Not that she was surprised. He'd experienced what could have been a life-changing ordeal. She was truly grateful she'd had the foresight to run for the sheriff. It was pure luck the former sheriff was there at the same time.

Just thinking about it made her shudder. "Are you alright?" Dennis asked. He didn't say much most of the time, but when he did, he was usually checking that *she* was doing alright.

Rachel smiled tentatively. "Just thinking about yesterday. I'm truly sorry."

Dennis stiffened. "You are not responsible for your father's actions," he said firmly. "If that were the case, you would already be incarcerated along with your criminal father. I think we have enough for now," he said, suddenly changing the subject. "Once these shelves are refilled, we can come back and assess another section." Without another word, he turned away and strode to the storeroom.

She'd upset him, that much was clear. Suddenly Rachel understood why. They'd been busy, and his mind was elsewhere. Her words reminded him of his horrific ordeal. He was helpless at the hands of her father, but daily, he was the one in charge. That must have affected him greatly.

She hurried after Dennis, and once in the storeroom, gathered up the required stock. Dennis had a trolley which he'd already partially filled and allowed Rachel to do the rest. His demeanor told her he was repentant, but he had nothing to apologize for.

They silently refilled the shelves and continued until the store was back in its original state.

"Thank you for your help today, Rachel," Dennis said when everything was again in order.

Was he dismissing her? He reached into the cashbox and handed her two dollars. "I don't want your money," she said firmly. "I told you that this morning."

He studied her for close to a minute. "I know, but your help has been invaluable. Would you…" Dennis rubbed a hand across his chin. She'd watched him do that a few times today. Usually when he was pondering a problem. "Are you available to work for me tomorrow?"

She studied him this time.

"I'd like to employ you on a casual basis," he quickly added. "We can assess it each day if that works for you."

Rachel silently weighed up his offer. The money sat loosely in her hands. She wanted to throw it back at him, but knew it would offend Dennis greatly. They didn't know each other well, but they'd worked closely today, and Rachel felt she'd come to know him.

When she was ready to move on, after the court case, whenever that may be, she would need money. "That sounds good. Thank you." Rachel closed her fist around the two-dollar note.

Dennis looked her up and down, then screwed up his face. "Your clothes are a mess. I apologize for not outfitting you correctly this morning." He strode into the storeroom and returned with a package, which he held onto. "It's an apron. Working in the store can be dirty work." He grinned then. "Even I use an apron."

Rachel glanced at the leather apron tied around his waist. She hadn't taken any notice of it earlier. She reached for the apron.

"Might as well leave it here," he said. "I'll put it behind the counter for you."

"Thank you. What time would you like me to start in the morning?"

"Is eight too early for you? I close at six, but you can leave earlier if you prefer."

Her heart pounded. Rachel could already count the dollars adding up for her relocation to some place no one knew her. She would take all the work she could get. "Eight until six. Got it," she said, then headed toward the door. As the bell tinkled over her head, she lifted a hand and waved.

For the first time in many years, her heart was full of happiness.

Rachel sat in the parlor of the preacher's house sipping tea.

"It sounds like you had a busy day," Faith said after Rachel had recalled her day. "When you left this morning, I expected you back soon after." She pierced Rachel with her eyes. "You were convinced Dennis wouldn't forgive you."

"You told me there was nothing to forgive. Dennis told me the same thing."

Clyde spoke up then. "Dennis can be arrogant, but he is a good person. It's a matter of getting to know the real person behind the gruff exterior."

Faith agreed.

Rachel glanced from one to the other. "I didn't see that side of him at all. He taught me whatever was required, and we worked together well. Ethel Bowman had a school visit with her senior students in the afternoon, and it was extremely busy. I was pleased to help."

The pair exchanged glances.

She wasn't sure what that was about, but it piqued her curiosity. "I made lunch for Dennis. He seemed to enjoy it."

Again, glances were exchanged. Rachel wasn't sure what they were thinking, but whatever it was, they had no intention of telling her. Perhaps Dennis had a reputation for not eating properly? Yes, that had to be it.

She would ensure on the days she worked, Dennis was well-fed. A hardworking man like Dennis needed to eat well. Otherwise, how did he get through the day? That thought made Rachel wonder what he ate for supper. She could cook his evening meal too, if that helped him.

All these plans she was making for Dennis, and she didn't know if he was interested. Either way, it was exciting to think she could assist him. Especially after what her father almost did to him.

The vision of Dennis lying dead behind the counter flashed before her, and Rachel knew she'd saved his life. In exchange, he had probably saved hers.

Chapter Seven

At eight o'clock precisely, Dennis opened the blind to the store window and unlocked the door. To his surprise, Rachel was standing outside, waiting to come in. He pulled the door wide open to let her inside. "Good morning," he said cordially. "I do hope you haven't been waiting long."

"Not long," she said, then ducked her head. Dennis wasn't convinced.

"Next time, knock when you arrive. It can get quite brisk outside in the mornings."

Rachel nodded, but said nothing. Once inside, he retrieved the apron he'd put aside for her. "This will protect your clothes. I'm truly sorry for not thinking about it yesterday."

"It was nothing more than a little dust," she said, waving his words aside. "But thank you for the apron. I appreciate it."

Dennis handed over the apron, and their hands brushed. His fingers tingled. Rachel glanced up at him. She couldn't have felt that—it was all in his imagination. "I restocked the shelves after the store closed last night," he told her, and Rachel appeared shocked.

"Again?" she asked, her voice sounding flabbergasted.

"It's a constant struggle." Dennis walked behind the counter, and Rachel followed. They'd been there for mere minutes when customers streamed through the door. "Good morning," Dennis said collectively.

"Good morning," Rachel said, echoing his greeting. He liked this arrangement and wondered exactly how long he would have her services. Perhaps he should visit the sheriff's office to check if they had a court date yet.

A tinkle over the door interrupted his thoughts. "Good morning, Faith. What can I do for you today?" Dennis asked, then reached for her written list.

"Thank you, Dennis," she said, then smiled at her house guest. Of course she would. Rachel was staying with her and the preacher. Rachel was busy with another customer, so Dennis worked at fulfilling Faith's small order. It wasn't long before she left the store.

Rachel leaned back in relief once the store was cleared of customers. "You seem to get bursts of customers, then a lull. Isn't that strange?" she asked warily.

"You're right," he told her. "I think perhaps they see their friends coming in and follow suit. I believe the butcher shop sees similar patterns. Allie has told me the diner has it happen too. None of us are complaining."

They set to work restocking the shelves that were again depleted. As they did so, the bell tinkled. Both Rachel and Dennis glanced up to see the sheriff. Dennis's heart pounded. Was the sheriff here to say they were releasing Rachel's father? For both their sakes, he hoped not.

Dennis strode toward the front counter. Rachel followed suit. "Good morning, Sheriff. What can I do for you?" he asked, trying not to sound worried.

"Morning, Dennis, Miss Dougherty." He tipped his hat to Rachel, then suddenly pulled it off and brushed his hair back with his fingers. "I came by to say the judge won't be here for another two weeks. Could be more. Says he has a long list at Helena." Tommy Garrett shrugged then. "We would all like it over with quickly, but it's out of my control."

Rachel seemed to wilt in front of his eyes. Dennis moved closer and put an arm around her shoulder. She glanced up at him but didn't protest. She wasn't the only one to notice, Sheriff Garrett clearly noticed, and raised both eyebrows at Dennis. It made him aware of the liberty he'd taken when he had no right.

"That means you can work here for longer," Dennis said, trying to make light of the announcement. "I'm sure that will help with your income." Rachel gasped, and Dennis immediately felt bad. "I didn't mean…"

"No, it's alright," she replied. "You are right. I have no money of my own, except what you gave me yesterday. My father controlled all the money." Her face stiffened. "Money he stole. Please excuse me," she said, then hurried toward the kitchen.

"Is she alright?" Tommy asked.

Dennis stared at the sheriff. "Did she look alright?" Then he stormed off, leaving the other man alone in the store. Moments later he heard the bell, so assumed he'd left. "Rachel," he said quietly, trying not to startle her.

She was checking the water level in the kettle, then placed it back on the stove. Next, she took two clean mugs from the rack on the sink. "Coffee for you?" she asked.

Nodding, Dennis stepped toward her. "I apologize for taking liberties earlier."

"No harm done," she said, then frowned. "What would you like for lunch? I need to plan."

His heart hammered. Rachel certainly was looking after him, but then she would be gone in two weeks, or maybe a little longer. What was he to do then? "Anything works for me. Take whatever you need from the store. If you need anything from the butcher's store, grab some money from the cash tin."

She stared at him, seemingly startled at his words. "It's one thing to take items from the store, and I'm more than happy to go to the butcher's, but are you certain?"

"I'm certain," he said.

A smile came to her face. Did that give her more freedom with her cooking? Dennis guessed he would find out later. Rachel poured his coffee and placed it on the table. "Would you like me to get some cookies from the store?" she asked.

Cookies? How long had it been since he'd been spoiled like this? His mind ticked over trying to remember—it would be when his dear mother was alive. She had passed many years ago. His father too. Dennis didn't want to think sad thoughts right now. Rachel made him happy.

That thought gave him pause. It had to be because she'd made his life easier. And she was making good food for him.

She made a small pot of tea, then placed it on a small board on the table, along with her empty mug. "Was that a no for cookies?" She stared at him, her face blank.

"It's a yes," he said, then grinned.

Rachel smiled.

"I haven't had cookies for years," he added, and her smile suddenly faded.

Reaching for a plate, Rachel hurried out of the kitchen and returned a short time later. "I wasn't sure what flavors you liked, so I brought a mixture."

Dennis's heart fluttered. He really needed to see the doc. What would Rachel do if he collapsed in a heap in front of her?

"Dennis? Are you alright?" she asked as she poured her tea.

The store was quiet, which meant as soon as they started their break, it would be busy again.

"You don't have many breaks from the store, do you?" Rachel asked.

"Never. Until yesterday, that is." Dennis lifted his mug and thought about that. He spent all day every day at the store. He woke at dawn and sorted out the ledgers. The store opened at eight, and he worked through until six. Then he restocked the shelves, often until late into the night. "My entire life is centered around my business." Sadness overtook him. Why hadn't anyone asked him that before?

Rachel had noticed after only one day. Then again, several of the townsfolk had mentioned his long hours. Perhaps Dennis hadn't wanted to listen to them. Rachel was different—she seemed to understand him. And she wanted to help him.

He wanted to help her, too.

Dennis shook himself mentally. He didn't help people. He'd always believed he wasn't a bad person, but admitted he could be selfish. More than anything, he looked out for himself. With no one else to worry about, he only had himself to care for. Since Rachel came into his life, everything changed.

When she left, his life would go back to the way it was before. Dennis's heart thudded. Was that really what he wanted?

Chapter Eight

Rachel stared at Dennis from across the table. She felt sad for him. The man was lonely and had pushed himself into a shell. From what she gathered, he was slowly coming out of that shell with her presence here at the store.

It appeared they were two peas in a pod. She could never be herself. Her father forced her to comply with what he wanted, never abiding by her wishes. She couldn't even speak unless he gave his permission.

He murdered her mother for speaking up when he told her to keep quiet. Faith told Rachel it had taken real courage to run for the sheriff. She was right. Bart would have easily, and unblinking, shot her in the back as she ran. Her heart pounded to the point she'd almost fainted as she ran away. Luckily for Rachel, he was distracted by Dennis.

It had allowed her to get help. Faith said she could easily have run and hidden until he'd finished with Dennis, but Rachel couldn't allow that to happen.

His death would have been on her conscious, knowing she could have prevented it.

"Rachel?" Dennis asked, then reached across the table and touched her hand before she answered.

She was startled at the unexpected touch. "Sorry, I was thinking."

"Good things, I hope," he told her.

Rachel shook her head. His eyes looked sad. Before either of them spoke again, the bell over the door tinkled. "I'll go," Rachel told him. "You stay here and rest." She hurried out to the store before he had a chance to protest.

"Good morning," Rachel greeted the customer, not knowing her name. "I'm Rachel—I'm helping Dennis in the store."

The older woman smiled. "Mildred Cavendish," she said as she clasped a long list. Leaning in a little closer, she told Rachel, "Molly, the doctor's wife is my daughter, and Joey is my grandson." By now she was beaming, and it was obvious she was a proud mother and grandmother.

"How wonderful," Rachel said. "I'm new to town, so I'm still getting to know everyone." She reached out a hand for the list Mrs. Cavendish held. "Are you coming back for your shopping or waiting?" It was a comprehensive list, so would take a while.

"I have an appointment with the dressmaker, so I will come back if that is alright with you?" She appeared a little anxious and Rachel wanted to put her at ease.

"Let me check this list, but I think we have you covered." She ran her eyes down the paper, and everything seemed in order. She smiled when she came across *candy stick*, knowing that would be for the small boy. "Any particular candy stick?" Rachel asked, a smile tugging at her lips.

"Any kind will do. It's a treat for little Joey. If all is well, I'll be on my way. I'm not sure how long I will be." She beamed again. "Today is measuring and choosing fabrics. I'm updating my Sunday best," she said, leaning in again. "It hasn't been my best for a while now."

Mrs. Cavendish quickly left the store and headed toward the dressmaker's store.

Rachel looked down at her own gown. It had been a long time since she'd had new clothes. There were a select few Bart made her wear to make store owners feel comfortable with her before moving in to attack. Ragged clothing did not breed acceptance, he always said. Not that she had many gowns.

Faith had loaned her several gowns to use while she was in town. Her new friend was not only gracious, but she was a true Christian. Rachel prayed she would be like Faith one day. Not the daughter of a gunslinger and murderer.

She closed her eyes against the tears that threatened to fall, then quickly opened them in case Dennis came out and found her upset. Rachel reached for a large box and began to fulfill Mrs. Cavendish's order—flour, oats, sugar, and molasses. She wondered if Dennis added items to the account as he went or later with a big order like this. Moments later, he stood nearby.

"What do you have there?" he enquired, looking far more relaxed than he had earlier. Stopping to rest mid-morning seemed to do him good. He glanced at the paper in her hand. "Ah, Mrs. Cavendish has been in."

"How did you… Oh, the candy stick!"

Dennis grinned. "Every order there's a candy stick for little Joey. We can tackle this together," he said. "For a big order like this one, I usually get the supplies from the storeroom." He pointed to the quantities. Dennis was right. Every item was the biggest size. "Mrs. Cavendish only comes into town once or twice a month, so she's usually buying for a month at a time."

Rachel's heart thudded. How did she miss that? Interpreting flour as a small bag suddenly seemed ridiculous. According to Dennis, and he would know, the bulk size Dennis bought was the size she purchased.

"They live on a ranch, and have several cowpokes," he told her. "They have chickens and a cow, plus a vegetable patch, so they're self-sufficient in that way. Everything else the Cavendish's get here in town. The bulk of it from my store."

She enjoyed hearing about their customers. It made her feel part of the community, only she wasn't. And they weren't their customers, they were Dennis's customers. Still, there was no reason she couldn't pretend while she was here. Was there?

They worked side by side, completing the order, ticking off each item as they placed it in the large box. "When I'm done, I'll use Mrs. Cavendish's list to add everything to her account," Dennis explained. "It's a far better use of time doing it that way."

Rachel smiled. Dennis had a sound business head. He'd discovered what worked and what didn't, and implemented that into his business. However, he hadn't found a way to give himself time outside his business. Perhaps in the short time she would be in Crystal Springs, she could help him see that.

"Last of all," Dennis said, reaching into the candy jar, "is a candy stick for little Joey. I don't charge her for this, but I don't think she's ever realized."

He grinned momentarily, then his grin faded. It had Rachel wondering what was going on in his mind.

She studied him, but couldn't help but ask. "Is everything alright, Dennis? You seem suddenly…sad."

His eyes stared back at her and he shook his head. "Don't mind me. I just wondered what it would be like to have a family. Someone who loved you the way Mrs. Cavendish loves her family."

Rachel swallowed back the emotion his words evoked. "You have an entire town who loves you. I've only been here a short time, but it's already clear they see you as family."

Dennis frowned, but said nothing. She already felt as though they were friends. He was a good man and deserved happiness. If only he would get over his stubbornness of working all hours of the day and night.

She only had two weeks, but Rachel was determined to mold him into someone who loved his personal life as much as his work life. Or indeed, had a personal life.

Chapter Nine

Dennis carried Mrs. Cavendish's purchases out to the wagon. "Joseph could have done that," she protested, even as they had almost reached the wagon.

"I'm young and strong," he told his best customer. "I truly don't mind." He glanced about. "Where is he? Am I going to miss him today?"

"At the bootmaker's. Those old boots he refuses to discard have finally fallen apart." She laughed, and it was clear Joseph's wife was beyond happy about the situation. "Ah, here he comes now," she said, and watched as her husband approached them.

"Dennis, my boy," Joseph said. "Thank you for your help. Have you found a wife yet?"

It was all Dennis could do not to roll his eyes. "I keep telling everyone I'm not looking."

"Take it from an old man who used to work himself to death," Joseph said, his voice firm and his expression serious. "Work won't be there for you when you are old and gray. It won't help when you fall down, and it won't bring you the best chicken soup either." He turned to his wife and winked.

Dennis squinted. Was there some conspiracy going on? Lately, everyone he met was urging him to marry. It was making him think he needed to find a wife. He knew it wasn't as simple as that. "I haven't found the right person," he said firmly. His own words made him shudder.

Joseph slapped a hand on his back. "How do you find the right person when you lock yourself away in that store every waking hour?"

The question made him pause. It was like a lightning bolt to his heart. Joseph was right, and Rachel had been telling him the same thing about the store. Dennis knew he had to make some changes in his life. How he did that was another thing altogether.

He glanced from Mrs. Cavendish to Joseph. "You're right. Everyone tells me the same thing— get a wife, they all keep saying."

"You've arranged marriages for many of the townsfolk," Mrs. Cavendish told him. "Perhaps it's time for us to do the same for you."

Without another word, Joseph helped his wife into the wagon. He shook Dennis's hand, then leaned in. "Think about what I said, my boy. Life is short—

you only get one chance at it. Love and family are far more important than work."

Soon they were gone, but Joseph's words were embedded in Dennis's mind. He was right—it wouldn't be long before Dennis would turn forty. Less than two years away. Did he want to live the rest of his life like this? Even Rachel, a complete stranger until two days ago, had insisted he worked too much.

He spun around and headed into the store. Dennis had a lot to think about, but even if he decided to marry, who would become his wife? The choices were few in Crystal Springs. Besides, most of the townsfolk didn't have a lot of time for him. He'd heard the gossip—they all thought he was arrogant.

They hadn't guessed the truth, that deep down he was shy and lonely. Except for church, the store was his only outlet for talking to people.

The aroma wafting from the kitchen to the store was enticing. Rachel was a breath of fresh air. She was a hard worker, the customers loved her, and she was a terrific cook. Dennis might not have known her long, but he was quickly becoming enamored with her.

He stopped in his tracks. What he meant was he liked her. Yes, that was it. Being a hard worker had appealed to him from the start. Of course, he recoiled when her father had pulled a gun on him, but she'd protested from the start. She'd pleaded with him to stop. That told Dennis she wasn't part of the plan.

The store was empty of customers, which was a pleasant change. Even when it wasn't, Rachel was there, helping him out. He was truly enjoying having her help him. It gave him time to write up the ledgers during the day, which meant he didn't have to spend his free time at night. Lately, he'd neglected his reading. Especially his Bible reading. It had always been part of his nightly routine, but was sadly lacking of late.

Having Rachel there had showed Dennis what he was missing—time to himself. Was it any wonder the townsfolk had little time for him except to buy from his store? Would that also suffer as a result? He hoped it wouldn't.

Rachel slipped into the kitchen, where he was tending to the ledgers. "Would you like another coffee?" she asked.

He glanced up and smiled. Dennis never thought he would enjoy having a woman in his kitchen. Or his home. The smile quickly faded as he remembered this was only a temporary situation. Soon Rachel would be gone. She vowed to leave town once the court case was over.

Could he convince her to stay on at the store? That way, she would have a job to keep her here. Wasn't that the reason she'd given him for leaving, anyway?

Dennis shook himself mentally. He was being selfish. The entire reason she'd decided to move on was to have anonymity. Move to a town where no one knew her and judged her on her father's sins.

Wasn't that already happening? Almost everyone in Crystal Springs who had met her understood she was helpless to stop her thieving father. That Rachel herself was also a victim of his criminal activities.

And yet, here she was, working in the store as though she hadn't a care in the world.

She was a strong woman, Dennis couldn't deny her that. Perhaps he should consider her as a candidate for marriage.

Shocked at his own thoughts, Dennis closed the ledger and took up Rachel's offer. "Coffee would be wonderful. Thank you."

She smiled and filled the mug she had already prepared. "I made cake this morning," she explained as she placed a thick slice of cake in front of him, along with the mug of steaming hot coffee.

A man could definitely get used to this.

Chapter Ten

A few days had passed, and a feeling of contentment washed over Rachel. Never had she felt so wanted, so needed, or so revered in her life. Why people viewed Dennis as arrogant, she wasn't sure. Perhaps he'd never let anyone really get to know him.

Working side by side as they did, she'd discovered the real Dennis. The kind man, the patient man, and a man willing to forgive her sins. Even if those sins truly belonged to her father.

Dennis glanced up and smiled. Her heart fluttered, and suddenly warmth filled her entire being. Rachel already knew she was getting far too close to her employer. She had fooled herself into thinking they were more than that. It felt more like they were...dare she even think it? Married.

The only difference was Rachel left the store at night and came back in the mornings. How she wished it could be different. She wasn't foolish enough to think any man would want someone like her. Besides, Dennis was a confirmed bachelor. Everyone told her so.

Rachel shook herself mentally. She'd allowed herself to be lulled into a false sense of security. Once her father's court case was over—and he would be convicted, there was no doubt—she would have enough money to leave town and set up a home where no one knew her.

The experience she'd had here at the mercantile would place her in good stead for a position in another mercantile, in another town. This time, she wouldn't place herself in a position where her feelings would rule her heart.

"I enjoy having you here, Rachel," Dennis suddenly said as he sipped his coffee.

Her heart fluttered. Did he want more?

"I know you want to leave town, but you've been so helpful and made my life far easier. Would you consider making it permanent?"

Disappointment hit her. With her heart pounding, Rachel knew she had to answer. "I…" It was an excellent offer. Perhaps she should accept. "I'd have to think about it. But thank you," she said, then turned away to stir the stew she had cooking for his supper.

"That stew sure smells good. What am I going to do if you leave town?" he asked with a chuckle.

Rachel knew he was trying to make light of his question and not make her feel guilty, but she felt bad. She felt as though she was letting him down and knew she could easily stay. If she did, what of her plans?

She spun around to face him again. "I'll think about it," she told him, then left the kitchen when the bell over the door tinkled.

As she made her way into the store, Rachel glanced about. It might not belong to her, but it felt like home. Dennis felt far more than he truly was. It seemed they belonged together, and if it hadn't been for fate, and her murderous father, they would never have met.

Rachel reminded herself yet again that Dennis was not interested in marriage. And why would he be? Employing her meant he had the best of both worlds—someone to help in the store and prepare his meals. Heck, she even cooked breakfast for him when she arrived each morning.

Sure, he protested daily, but not once had he refused to eat the meal. Rachel was an excellent cook, and she knew it. Mother was the best cook she'd ever come across, and she taught Rachel everything she knew.

"Good afternoon," she said as a small group of women came into the store. "How may I help you today?" Dennis joined her moments later, and a shiver went up her spine.

Rachel hoped she wasn't coming down with something. The last thing she needed was to get sick. Especially when she was saving up to move on to another town.

Faith stared at her from across the parlor. "You said you'd think about it?" She sighed. "I thought you enjoyed working at the mercantile?"

Clyde sat quietly listening to the conversation with baby Elsie on his knee, but didn't interrupt. They had both been so kind and generous to her, and refused to allow Rachel to pay them board. These two, this family, along with people like Dennis, made her want to rethink her stance on leaving town.

"I do, it's just," Rachel didn't know how to explain it. "People here know my affiliation with Bart Dougherty. I would prefer not to be connected to him in any way." There, she'd said it. Now she hoped they would understand. "I still cannot understand why my mother would marry a man like that." Rachel stared down at her hands, then shook her head. "I shouldn't have said that. My mother was a gentle soul—he is the complete opposite, and has been for as long as I can remember."

Clyde studied her, then frowned. He never said much, and Rachel had come to realize that was the way he was. Until he needed to speak. Then it was a different story.

"How far back do you remember him?" he suddenly asked.

Rachel's eyes opened wide in amazement. "I can't recall anything about him until I was around four, maybe five. Why do you ask?"

Clyde waved a hand in front of himself. "No reason, just curious. I'm interested in family matters, that's all."

Faith glanced at him, then pivoted back to Rachel. "You will consider Dennis's offer, won't you?" she asked gently.

"I will, but no promises," Rachel said.

Faith seemed sad about the prospect of her leaving. Rachel felt the same way. "I guess it's more about a clean break and starting life afresh."

"Everyone in town will miss you, especially Dennis, I'm certain," Faith said. Rachel couldn't decipher the expression she wore.

"I will miss it here, too. Everyone has been so kind. None more so than you and Clyde. And Dennis, of course. He's taught me so much about working in the mercantile. Even how to order from the suppliers."

She rang her hands in her lap. Saying it out loud forced Rachel to realize what she'd be leaving behind. Already she had a good job and caring friends. Why would anyone refuse such a wonderful offer?

Clyde suddenly spoke up. "We want you to know, Faith and I, you can stay here for as long as you want."

Not that it surprised Rachel. They were decent people, but she couldn't continue to impose on them if she stayed. "I couldn't do that. You have your own family and need your privacy." What Rachel wouldn't give to have a proper family. Despite thinking it, she couldn't voice her wishes.

"You are the one who would suffer a loss of privacy," Clyde told her. "We have Bible Study, Ladies Auxiliary, and other groups that meet here regularly." He smiled at her. "We'd love to have you stay. Please don't discount staying for that reason."

Clyde glanced across at Faith, as he often did. They seemed to have some sort of silent communication between them. Rachel prayed that one day she would have what they enjoyed. But was certain it was a rarity and something she'd never experience.

Rachel stood. "If you don't mind, I'm going to retire for the night. I have work tomorrow."

"Goodnight," Faith said. "Think about what we've discussed. You are one of the townsfolk now. There's really no need for you to leave." Rachel didn't answer and Faith continued. "You have a good job and a home where you are loved and wanted. People here love you, too."

She came to Rachel and hugged her tightly. The last time anyone hugged her other than Faith was when her mother was alive. Tears rolled down Rachel's cheek. She missed her mother greatly. Why did Bart have to hit this town, of all the places he could have robbed?

People here were special—they made a person feel they mattered. All her life, Bart had told her she was useless and had to make up for that. His way of doing that was using her as bait for his robberies. Not that she did anything. Rachel couldn't bring herself to do so.

Soon she was sobbing, and her mind was whirling. Clyde joined them and put an arm around her. He said a prayer, asking for a guiding hand to make her decision. The three of them stood silently for what seemed to be hours. Rachel knew it was only minutes, but during that time, a peacefulness came over her.

For the first time in years, Rachel knew she was wanted, and she was loved. Now she needed to do something about it.

Dennis sat on the wooden bench outside the store, waiting for Rachel's arrival. It was a first for him. Usually he waited inside, but today he was eager to find out if she was staying.

Not that she'd promised an answer today, because she hadn't.

She glanced up and gasped as she noticed him there. "Is everything alright, Dennis?" she asked as she approached. Instead of going inside, she sat down beside him. It was something they'd never done before.

Rachel kept herself a safe distance from him. Propriety demanded it, he figured. Oh, how he despised propriety! "That depends," he said quietly, ensuring no one else could hear. Not that anyone was nearby, but one never knew. "Have you come to a decision?"

"About accepting the position here at the store?" She frowned. It didn't bode well for the answer he wanted to hear. "I've given it a lot of thought. I've even discussed it with Faith and Clyde."

"I hope they convinced you to stay on." His heart thudded. Perhaps they could show her the benefits of staying in Crystal Springs. Suddenly, Dennis realized pressuring her was not helping. "It's totally up to you," he said, then stood.

Without thinking, Dennis reached out to help Rachel to her feet. She hesitated for a heartbeat, then clasped his hands. A shiver went through him, and his heart fluttered.

As Rachel came to an upright position, they were almost face-to-face. She was so close he could feel her warm breath on his face. Her lips were so close to his, Dennis was tempted to kiss her, but that wouldn't be right. Especially not out here, where everyone could see. He restrained himself from glancing about to check if anyone was around.

The fragrance she wore wound its way into his nostrils and into his memory. It was the same one she wore each day. Dennis adored it. When she moved from one spot to another, he could still enjoy it for several moments. It often made him smile.

"I suppose we should go inside now." Rachel's sweet voice cut through his musings. Then she cleared her throat and glanced down. Dennis still held her hands in his, and if he was honest, he didn't want to let them go. Reluctantly, he did.

"Ah, Dennis, Rachel. Good morning to you both. Isn't it a touch brisk to be outside this early?" Trust Allie to notice. "I came by to collect my weekly order. It has arrived, hasn't it?"

The interruption was what he needed. His mind had become befuddled. Along with the heart fluttering, he was sure something dire was going on with him. "It certainly has," Dennis told her, focusing on Allie rather than Rachel. "It's also packed and ready to go. I'll deliver it shortly if that works for you. Rachel can manage without me." He turned to Rachel and smiled. How did he ever cope without her? His heart sank. How would he survive when she left?

Dennis knew there was a more pressing question— would his heart ever be the same without Rachel in his life? He knew he needed to do something about it, and that didn't mean pressuring her to work in the store. It wasn't about working together. From his perspective, their relationship had grown into far more than that.

"Thank you. I'll leave you both to it, then. Have a good day, both of you." Allie spun around and headed back to the diner. She worked hard and worked long hours. She relied on supplies from his store, and for that, Dennis was grateful.

He opened the door and let Rachel enter ahead of him. Then he went straight to the storeroom and retrieved Allie's order, which was already packed and waiting on the trolley he kept for that very reason.

Of course, he'd rather be here with Rachel, but he had work to do. And customers to keep happy. Over the past week or so, he'd learned there was more to life than work. He'd also learned there was only one person he wanted to spend his days with, and she was already within his grasp. Why he hesitated to do anything about making it permanent, except for offering her a job, he didn't know.

But Dennis did know—he knew nothing about matters of the heart. Perhaps it was time he learned.

Dr. Marcus Ryan sat behind his desk and studied Dennis. It was very obvious he was trying not to smirk. "Unbutton your shirt. I need to listen to your heart," he said, then came to stand behind Dennis.

This was new for Dennis. He was as healthy as a horse—he rarely saw a doctor. Marcus had checked him over after the attack, but he was fine except for what Marcus called shock. And who wouldn't be after what happened?

"Your heart is fine, as I suspected. Explain to me again when you get this fluttering sensation."

Dennis re-buttoned his shirt. Then he thought hard. "I hadn't noticed it until a couple of days after Rachel started working at the mercantile. It's happened a lot since then." He glanced up at Marcus, who seemed to concentrate hard as he wrote some notes.

"And it's only been happening since Rachel arrived?" Marcus studied him.

Suddenly, a thought occurred to Dennis. "Do you think her perfume could be affecting me?" Marcus grinned, then moved his hand to cover his mouth. It was perplexing, to say the least.

Suddenly, Marcus became deadly serious. It worried Dennis. "No, I don't think it's her perfume. There is nothing wrong with your heart either— you're as strong as an ox, always have been." The doctor leaned forward and opened his mouth. Then promptly closed it again.

Dennis's heart thudded. "You can tell me, Doc. What's wrong with me?" It was serious, he could tell. The doc's demeanor was scaring him.

Marcus came back around to the patient side of his desk. Silently, he sat on the edge of the desk next to

Dennis. He lifted a hand and put it to Dennis's shoulder. "Dennis, my friend, I have a diagnosis for you. You are in love."

Dennis was prepared for anything, but not that.

Chapter

Twelve

Rachel was worried. Dennis had left more than half an hour ago to deliver Allie's order and hadn't returned. She thought about closing the store and reporting him missing to the sheriff, but didn't want to embarrass him if he'd merely gone off for a walk.

She frowned. It was not like Dennis at all. He was diligent, he was hardworking, and never disappeared like this.

She glanced up as the bell over the door tinkled. Relief flooded her when he strolled through the door with his empty trolley. It was on her lips to ask where he'd been, but knew it wasn't her place.

"Any problems?" Dennis asked nonchalantly. If she didn't know better, Rachel would think he'd been gone ten minutes, and no more. He didn't bring up his disappearance, and neither would she.

"None," Rachel told him. "Are you alright, Dennis? You appear pale. Do you need to see the doctor?" She studied him further—he was as white as the sheets he sold in the store.

His head shot up and Dennis stared at her. "I don't need to see the doc. I'm healthy as an ox." He stormed off toward the storeroom with the trolley and returned a short time later.

"Coffee?" Rachel asked when he returned to the front of the store. Something was wrong, but she couldn't put her finger on it. "I have a fresh pot ready."

He smiled then. Perhaps he needed a break. Yes, that was it. Normally Dennis had coffee before the store even opened, but today he had been interrupted by taking Allie's order to her. Then... Well, then he disappeared into thin air.

Thankfully, he'd returned unscathed. If he wanted to tell her where he'd been, he would. It wasn't her business, and she had no right to ask. Rachel vowed not to pry into his private business.

"You are a true gem," Dennis said then. "I should probably have a cookie or two. I haven't eaten yet."

Rachel gasped. She couldn't help herself. "You've not had breakfast?" She asked, incredulous, then glanced at him briefly.

Of course he hadn't eaten – they'd been interrupted when Allie arrived. Her heart pounded and she slapped her hands to her mouth. "I apologize. It's not my place to tell you what to do." She was mortified. Who was she to tell her employer what to do? He may well rescind his offer of permanent employment now. Not that she'd decided to stay. It was a tough decision for her to make.

The pending court case had her on edge. Once it was over, her mind would no longer be in turmoil. At least Rachel prayed that would be the case.

When she glanced at Dennis again, he was grinning. "You're an excellent cook, Rachel. I truly appreciate the way you look after me."

Her eyes opened wide in astonishment. Any other day, Dennis might have grunted in response to her words. Not today. "The store has been quiet. Let me pour your coffee and… How do pancakes with fried potatoes and onions sound?"

"It sounds perfect," Dennis said.

His voice sounded different. Strained. Wherever he'd gone, it had shaken him to his core. The only time she'd seen Dennis stressed like this was after her father had attacked him. It was understandable.

This was not the same, and she may never know what caused him to be this way.

Instead of trying to analyze his behavior, Rachel headed into the kitchen. A mug of coffee was on the table, waiting for him by the time he got there. Potatoes were frying, along with the onions, and the kitchen was filled with a delicious aroma. She was mixing the pancakes when she heard his chair scrape along the floor.

She turned to face him. "It won't be long," she told him. "The potatoes are almost done."

He stared at her with the strangest look on his face, and Rachel wasn't sure what to do about it. "You don't look well, Dennis. Should I fetch the doctor?"

Her words had the color draining from his face. "I've already seen the doc today. I'm fine." His pale face suddenly went red, and Dennis appeared distraught at his revelation. He gulped down his coffee. Was he trying to cover his red face from her?

At least now she knew where he'd been. "Are you feeling poorly? Perhaps it's because you hadn't eaten." She poured the pancake mixture into another pan. Had she chosen any other food for his breakfast today, he'd be eating already, and she could sit and talk with him. It seemed that's what he needed.

Dennis was always happy to talk about work, but rarely spoke about himself or his feelings. He was a very private person—she'd learned that soon after working for him. "Your breakfast will be ready in a few minutes," she said, then turned away to flip the two pancakes already in the pan. Rachel continued until they were all cooked, then placed four pancakes on a large plate, along with the potatoes and onions. The remaining pancakes were added to a plate in the center of the table.

She refilled his coffee, then went to tend to a customer who'd arrived.

Instead of her mind being on the customer, it was firmly on Dennis. Was he so unwell he needed the doctor? Was it her fault for not agreeing to work for him?

"I think that's everything. Thank you, Rachel." Mrs. Hornsby took her supplies and left the store.

Although she still hadn't decided, Rachel knew she would miss this town and its people if she left. She would especially miss Clyde and Faith and their very special friendship. Most of all, she would yearn for Dennis.

Oh, she knew he was difficult in his own way, but he was a good man. Dennis wanted the best for his store and his customers. He never overpriced his stock and delivered at no charge. It was very unlike some towns she'd been in.

He was a good Christian man, and he had a very special place in her heart.

Rachel stumbled. It was a revelation she hadn't expected. Especially from herself. How long had she felt that way? Now she knew what her decision must be—leave Crystal Springs. Dennis had no such feelings for her, and Rachel had no intention of being humiliated with her feelings not returned.

Moments later, Dennis returned to the store. He stared at her, then rushed forward. "What happened?" he asked, his voice urgent. He snatched up a kitchen towel from behind the counter and put it to her chin. "You're bleeding," he whispered, his voice calmer now.

"Bleeding?" Rachel glanced down. Her apron was covered in blood. How could she not realize she'd harmed herself? Even the counter had blood on it. Her blood.

"Come on," Dennis said. "I'm closing the store and taking you to see Marcus."

It seemed she had no say in it.

Marcus studied her apron, then took Rachel into his office before other patients who were already waiting. "I can wait," she told him.

"No, you can't," Marcus said firmly. "You wait here, Dennis." He immediately laid her on the surgery bed and removed the kitchen towel. "How did this happen? It's deep." He pulled the kitchen towel back and had Rachel hold on to it. "You need stitches."

She sighed. "Stupidity. I wasn't thinking about what I was doing. Instead, I was thinking about…" She stopped abruptly. Rachel wasn't certain she wanted to divulge what had caused her accident.

Marcus frowned, but didn't push her to answer. "This is going to hurt a bit," Marcus said. "I need you to keep still until I'm finished."

Rachel winced as he cleaned the wound, then stitched her chin. What a fool she'd been. She'd done this to herself. Not thinking clearly was not a good way to be. She'd proven that.

"There, all done. You might want to take off that bloodied apron. It might shock some of the townsfolk to see you like that." Marcus covered her stitches with a dressing. "You need to keep this dry and come back in a few days for me to check it's healing properly."

"I will, I promise," Rachel told him.

Marcus studied her as she lay there. "There's a bruise on your forehead. You didn't mention you'd hit your head. Go home and rest for at least a few days. We don't want concussion to set in. Oh, and that bruise will change color over the next few days." He held her hand and helped Rachel down. "Anyway, what were you thinking about so deeply you fell down?"

"Stumbled. I am trying to decide whether to stay in Crystal Springs after the court case. Dennis offered me a permanent position at the store."

Marcus grinned. "That's good," he said, then led her to the waiting room.

Dennis was pacing the floor and stopped when he spotted her. "Thank goodness," he said, rushing toward her. "I was extremely worried."

"It's a few stitches, Dennis," Rachel said, forcing herself not to roll her eyes.

Dennis pulled her close and hugged her. Something he had never done before. Rachel didn't push him away.

They walked back to the store in silence. As they arrived, he noticed a group of people waiting for the store to open. Dennis shuddered as he unlocked the door. Memories of the last time he'd done that came to mind.

A gentle hand to his arm pushed his demons aside. He turned to see Rachel's worried face. He was the one who should be worried. She had been injured in his store, under his watch.

Besides, he cared far too much for her to see Rachel hurt. After these customers were dealt with, he would ensure the obstacle that caused her injury was removed.

He shoved the bloodied apron underneath the counter. Customers didn't need to be upset by the vision of Rachel's blood. It was upsetting enough for him. Dennis's eyes suddenly focused on the blood on the counter. It wasn't a huge amount, but it was there. He pulled a box of candy over the top of it. He'd had it there, ready to refill the jar.

Rachel studied him as he fiddled. It was unlike him, and he knew it. Apparently, so did she. Of all the people in town, she knew him the best. She was also the one person who had known him the least amount of time. His heart fluttered again. This time, it made him smile.

Dennis now understood exactly what his fluttering heart meant, thanks to Marcus. When he'd seen Rachel standing there dazed and bleeding, his heart was hollow. He was certain he was going to lose her. Thanks to his quick thinking, he'd stemmed the blood, and got her the treatment she needed. She might not have believed it necessary, but Dennis knew it was.

Waiting for her at the doctor's office was pure agony. He'd been more worried than he could remember being in his entire life. Now he worried she would never forgive him, and would leave the store and the town forever.

Dennis prayed that didn't happen.

He glanced up to see Rachel helping a customer find an item. It gave him the opportunity to find whatever caused her to stumble. Only there was none. The broom was kept in the storeroom unless it was in use. He couldn't see it anywhere, which meant it was safely tucked away where it belonged. The trolley was also put away, and nothing sat on the floor.

He had strict rules about such things. They often had to hurry to help customers, which meant nothing was to be out of place. Not only behind the counter, but in the store itself. The same applied to the storeroom. He was perplexed, but it was a problem for another time.

"Is that everything, Beth?" Dennis asked his long-time customer. Beth and Wyatt were one of his success stories. Happily married after his intervention. It filled Dennis with pride.

"It is, thank you, Dennis. How is Rachel? I heard she had an accident." His heart thudded. Did the entire town know already? It hit him then that he was the one who normally spread such gossip. He didn't like it when the boot was on the other foot. Especially when it involved Rachel.

He vowed not to gossip ever again. Although Dennis knew that promise may not be an easy one to keep. He sighed. No wonder the townsfolk got so annoyed at him. If he saw himself through their eyes, he might feel the same.

He glanced across at his store assistant and smiled. "Rachel says she's fine. Needed a few stitches after a fall here in the store."

Beth gasped. "And she's still working?"

Dennis frowned. Beth had a point. "Perhaps you're right. I'll talk to her. Thank you. Good day to you, Beth."

As she was about to leave, Wyatt entered the store, a child on each arm. "I'm being pressured for candy," Wyatt said, a grin on his face.

Beth rolled her eyes. "Then I guess we need candy," she said, and turned back to Dennis. "Two pieces of candy, please, Mr. Andrews," she said, chucking each of their children under the chin. It warmed Dennis's heart to see the happy family, and he wanted that for himself.

"There you are," he said, handing a piece of candy to each of the youngsters. "No charge," he said, and Beth raised her eyebrows. He tried to ignore it. It might be a first, but he intended to ensure it wasn't the last time.

No more would he be hard-hearted Dennis, the storekeeper only interested in money. His heart had been opened up, and he knew he had to change his ways.

"Thank you, Dennis," Wyatt said, as his children wore big smiles. He then turned and left the store.

Warmth filled Dennis, and for once in his life, he knew the reason. He'd done something nice for no reason. Oh, he was never an ogre. That wasn't his style. But seeing those youngsters so happy because of him was a highlight of his day.

When the store cleared, he intended to talk with Rachel, send her home for the rest of the day. Beth knew more about such things than he did.

Finally, the store was void of customers, and he approached Rachel. "Can we talk?" he asked gently. "Perhaps in the kitchen."

She frowned, but hurried ahead of him. Rachel was sitting at the table, her brow creased with worry. "Is this because I haven't accepted your offer?" she asked quietly, as her hands twisted on the tabletop.

"Not at all," Dennis said, trying to put her mind at ease. "I think you should go home and rest for the remainder of the day. You've had quite a fall." She sighed in what appeared to be relief. "I will pay your wages, of course. So you won't lose money."

"I'm not worried about money," she said. "I don't want to let you down. We both know you need the help."

She was worried about him. Dennis thought that was sweet. His hand reached across the table to try and stop her hands twisting. It seemed clear to him she was upset about the entire situation, as she should be. No one should come to harm in his store. "You're not letting me down. I..." he wasn't sure how to say this, so simply blurted it out. "I can't find what caused you to stumble. Do you know what happened?"

Rachel bit her lip. "I was thinking and not looking where I was going."

He sighed in relief. "I'm glad."

Rachel frowned. "You're glad I fell?"

"Of course not! I'm glad I didn't cause it. I couldn't live with myself if my actions did this to you." He squeezed her hand and didn't want to ever let go. "Rachel," he said with emotion in his voice. "I have to tell you something."

The bell over the door tinkled, and Rachel stood. She grabbed onto the table, and he rushed to her side. "You sit down and stay here," he demanded. "I'll see to the customer."

He didn't want to leave her alone. Rachel was clearly lightheaded. Why hadn't he thought to take her straight back home?

Faith stood at the front counter, a worried look on her face. "I heard Rachel was injured. Should she be here?"

"I've been trying to convince her to go home, but not having much luck. She fell and needed stitches."

He heard Faith's gasp, and it cut him to the core. Those who really loved Rachel were worried about her. So far, there were many people. Especially for someone who was new to town. "You are welcome to come out and help me convince her to leave."

Dennis stepped to the door and turned the sign to closed. He then locked the door. Rachel was far more important than customers who could easily wait a few minutes. Faith stared at him, a shocked look on her face. She knew him too well.

"Through here," he said, leading her out to the kitchen.

"Faith! Is everything alright? Where's baby Elsie?" Rachel was clearly worried, and that was the last thing Dennis wanted.

"Elsie is with Clyde. I heard you'd been hurt." Faith glanced at Dennis then. "I've come to take you home."

Rachel studied her, then turned to Dennis. "I told you I'm fine."

Dennis put both hands up in front of himself. "Faith came here under her own steam. I've been trying to get you to go home, and now I'm demanding it."

Rachel scowled. "Demanding it?" She tried to stand again but was unsteady on her feet. Dennis caught her before she could fall. "You are clearly unwell.

I'll help Faith get you home safely. You're not to come back until you are one hundred percent well."

"I'll make sure of it," Faith said.

Between them, Faith and Dennis walked Rachel home to the parsonage. He would have picked her up and carried her there, but he was certain Rachel would protest.

When she was safely home and he knew she was being cared for, Dennis opened the store again, but not until he'd cleaned the counter of her blood.

When he returned, Dennis glanced about. Something was missing. It didn't take long for him to realize it was Rachel. He'd grown more than fond of her, as Marcus had pointed out. What would he do if she truly did leave town?

His heart broke at the thought.

Chapter

Fourteen

Rachel crossed the road from the parsonage. She'd been home for almost three days. Faith had insisted, and so had Dennis. She'd been surprised when he arrived that first evening with a bunch of flowers. The most expensive of those he sold in the store. He'd also brought a box of chocolates for her.

Clyde had fought back a grin when he told her Dennis was there to see her. She'll never forget the look on his face. It confused her.

Once she entered the parlor, Dennis waited until she was comfortably seated. He then told her to take as much time as she needed, and not worry about her wages—he was covering it all. He left as quickly as he'd arrived, but Rachel appreciated him visiting, and his words.

As she approached, she noticed him sitting on the wooden bench outside the store, drinking coffee. Rachel cringed. By his own admission, Dennis made the worst coffee in town. He glanced up when he noticed her, placing his coffee mug under the seat.

"Good morning," he said, caution in his voice. "How are you feeling? Are you sure you're well enough to come back so soon?"

As she moved closer, he frowned. Rachel knew exactly what he'd seen. The almost black bruise on the side of her forehead. "Did the doc know about that?" he asked. Or should that be demanded?

"It was smaller then, and yes, he knew."

"Then he probably told you to rest."

Dennis was clearly annoyed with her, but it was too bad. He'd been working himself into a frenzy over her being injured, and it was the last thing she wanted. "I'll make you some decent coffee. Have you eaten?" she asked.

Dennis seemed grateful. Likely for the coffee. "I made toast. And coffee." He scowled then. "Neither were very good. The coffee was bitter, and I burned the toast." He chuckled then, and Rachel was relieved. Dennis chuckling wasn't a regular occurrence. Bending down, he picked up the coffee mug he'd put under the bench, then opened the door for her. "I missed you, Rachel," he said once they were inside.

She slowly turned to face him. Rachel felt fine, but if she turned her head too quickly, dizziness hit. "I still have to take it easy, but I'm fine to work."

Dennis scowled. "Go home, Rachel," he said firmly, but she ignored his demand. She was bored doing nothing, and much preferred to keep busy.

Rachel strolled past him and headed toward the kitchen, where she began making coffee. She reached up to get a clean mug, but lost her balance. Dennis was right behind her. His arms steadied her, and his warmth flooded her. "Let me," he said, and pulled the mug down without effort.

"Thank you," she whispered, then turned in his arms. She watched as he breathed in her fragrance.

"I really missed you, Rachel," he said, "but I think you should take more time off."

She shook her head, then regretted it. Her hands went to her head, and Dennis didn't miss it. He stared down into her face, his eyes met hers, and then they strolled down to her lips. She couldn't help but stare back. "I… I need to sit down," Rachel said, and Dennis helped her to the nearest chair.

Dennis didn't look happy. In fact, he was thunderous. He pulled out his pocket watch. "I don't think the doc is open yet, but I'm getting him, anyway." Before she could protest, Rachel heard the front door being locked. Then he was gone.

Marcus sat in the chair opposite. "Which part of rest for at least a few days didn't you understand?" he demanded. "Did you at least sleep most of the time you were home?"

"I did," Rachel said. "I'm fine now, though."

Dennis rolled his eyes at the same time the doc sighed. "I'm certain Dennis can do without you for another few days. Even if he can't, it's too bad." He checked her stitches while he was there, and redressed them.

"I'm glad you came and got me, Dennis. Rachel is in no state to be working." He packed up his medical bag, then stood. "Dennis and I will walk you home, Rachel. I don't want you back here until next week. I'm sure Dennis can cope without you until then. He's run the store alone for years."

"I don't want to let anyone down," Rachel said quietly. "Especially after what my father did to Dennis and this town." Tears flooded her eyes, but she fought them back.

Squatting to her level, Dennis spoke gently. "You are not your father. Everyone in Crystal Springs loves you." He glanced up at Marcus then, and the pair shared a look. Rachel didn't know what that was about. "No one blames you for what happened," he said, then helped Rachel to her feet.

"I can get home alone," she protested. "It is only across the street. You have to open the store."

She heard both men sigh this time. "No, I don't," Dennis said firmly. "You are far more important to me than the store will ever be."

Rachel stared at him. Her head was pounding, but did Dennis really say she was more important than his store? That couldn't be right. If only it was.

After escorting her back home, much to her disgust, Marcus ensured she went straight to bed, and the curtains were closed. He told her he was waiting in the parlor until Faith reported back to say she was in her nightgown and resting.

True to his word, that's what he did. Marcus even popped in to say he would return the next day to check on her. Apart from pre-empting her boredom, Rachel would miss little Elsie. Marcus ordered complete rest and for her to sleep in a darkened room with the door closed.

This time she promised to follow doctor's orders. These headaches she was getting were debilitating. It certainly wasn't something she wanted to live with for longer than necessary.

Besides, if she was home too long, Rachel knew she would miss Dennis. It was the entire reason she'd returned earlier than she knew she should have.

Her mind was in a whirl, but it was clear enough she realized if she missed him this much when he was only across the street, what would it be like if she left town altogether?

It was a problem she needed to ponder another time. For now, she needed to sleep.

Rachel was returning to work today. Marcus had stopped by last evening to let Dennis know he'd given her the all-clear. He warned if she was lightheaded at all she needed to be checked again. Head injuries could be dangerous, even fatal, Marcus said.

"Don't worry," Marcus told him. "I've given Rachel a complete check, and I can't see any signs of concussion now. Still," he said conspiratorially, "If you have easy work she could do for a few more days, I'd appreciate it."

Now Dennis sat on the wooden bench. It really wasn't that comfortable, he'd discovered, but he'd endure anything for Rachel. Especially after the terrible experience she'd suffered. He glanced up to see her closing the gate of the parsonage, a smile on her face. She hurried across the road, and he could see there was color back in her face. The bruise seemed to have gone, and she certainly looked happy.

He met her halfway across the road. "Welcome back," he said quietly, not wanting to cause another headache. Loud noises would do that, and bright lights, Marcus told him last week. Marcus also told him it was past time he told Rachel he loved her.

Last time he tried to do that, a customer interrupted him. This past week without her, Dennis had been closing the store for his lunch break. He had vowed to continue that practice, as it gave him some time to recover from the busy morning he'd had. It was mostly busy in the store throughout the day. Besides, once his customers were used to his new routine, they wouldn't even grumble.

It would also give him time to talk to Rachel. Heaven knew they couldn't do it any other time.

"This is new," she said as they reached the door. "Closed for lunch at noon. Reopen at one." She turned to face him, and Dennis wasn't sure if she thought it was a terrible idea. "I'm glad," she said instead. "It will give us, er, you, time to recover from the morning's hectic work."

Her words were not missed by Dennis. Did that mean she'd decided to stay on? He hoped and prayed it was true, but he wouldn't press her. Instead, he opened the door and ushered her inside.

Dennis handed her a brand-new apron. He discarded the other one, deciding blood was far too difficult to remove. She hurried into the kitchen and began to prepare coffee. Dennis could smell the aroma already. In his mind, anyway. He'd missed Rachel's coffee, but more than that, he'd missed her.

She reached up to pull the mugs down, and Dennis hurried across to help her. He really needed to place the mugs lower, but then he wouldn't have an opportunity to stand this close to Rachel. Turning her head to face him slightly, Rachel smiled. "I've got this," she whispered.

"Are you certain?" he whispered back.

Rachel turned and was now in his arms. It felt like déjà vu—they'd been in almost the same situation last week. Only then, Rachel was in the throes of a concussion. Today she had her wits about her, and she stared up into his face.

Dennis couldn't help but stare into her beautiful emerald green eyes. They'd pulled him in almost from the start. The color was almost startling, and so different to her father's eyes. Surely he would have remembered that?

"Dennis," she whispered, her voice even quieter than before. Her eyes worked their way down his face to his lips. In the peripheral, he noticed her hand lifting. Should she push him away, Dennis would comply. He would never force himself on a woman. Instead, her fingers went to his lips, then caressed his cheeks. A shudder ran through him.

His arms tightened around her, and he gently kissed her neck. Dennis felt Rachel shiver. "Are you sure this is what you want?" he asked, his voice husky and unrecognizable to Dennis.

"I'm sure," Rachel answered. "I love you, Dennis." Her words hung in the air. How could he not know the way she felt?

Dennis lifted his head and studied her. "I love you, too. I was going to tell you the other day, but we were interrupted."

"Of course," she said, and Dennis knew he'd done the right thing by setting up break times. The customers would eventually get used to it. He knew they would.

Rachel shifted in his arms. She licked her lips, and his head went slowly down. There was no sign she wanted him to stop, so he kissed her. At first, his lips brushed hers lightly. It felt good. Rachel didn't push him away, so Dennis kissed her again. This time, it was a real kiss.

Her arms went up his back, and he pulled her closer still. Dennis knew in that moment, he could live the rest of his life with this woman. He only hoped she felt the same way.

A knock at the front door had them pulling apart. "Customers," Rachel said breathlessly.

"They really are a nuisance," Dennis said, holding back a laugh. "You make the coffee, I'll see to the customers." He left the kitchen with a skip in his step. Dennis couldn't recall another time he'd ever done that.

He crossed the floor, opened the blind, and unlocked the door. "Good morning," he told Mrs. Hargreaves. "How can I help you today?"

She stared at him for what seemed forever. "Coffee beans," she said eventually. "The same beans you use—the aroma is enticing."

Dennis wanted to tell her the woman making the coffee was as well, but somehow refrained.

Rachel had insisted on making lunch, despite Dennis offering to take her to the diner. She would have none of it. She had a stew on the stove for his supper, although Dennis would far prefer to have Rachel dine with him.

Apparently, it was bad enough she worked in the store, but that was vaguely acceptable because he was her employer. Not to mention customers coming and going throughout the day. When he finished eating the delicious chicken soup and biscuits she'd made for their lunch, Dennis sat back in his chair.

He watched her every move—there was no doubt, he wanted to marry Rachel. The question was, did she want to marry him? "Rachel," he said warily. "I need to ask you something. Come and sit beside me."

"Is everything alright?" she asked, her expression one of caution.

"That's what I want to know. I have to ensure I haven't crossed a line. I'd like to make you more than an employee. But you must be willing to make Crystal Springs your home."

He reached for her dainty hand and covered it with his own. Dennis not only loved this woman with all his heart, he would protect her for the rest of her days.

Suddenly, he dropped to the floor in front of her. "Rachel," he said, his voice unsteady. "I know I'm not much of a catch, but will you marry me?"

Her eyes opened wide in astonishment. Did that mean she was going to refuse? Dennis's heart pounded so loud he was certain he wouldn't hear her answer, anyway.

#

##

"I…" Rachel was bewildered. It was only hours ago they'd declared their love for each other. Was it too soon to make a lifetime commitment? As she stared down into the face of the man she loved with all her being, Rachel knew it wasn't. "Of course I will!" she declared, tears pooling in her eyes.

To Rachel's surprise, Dennis jumped up and pulled her from the chair. He enveloped her in his arms and held her so tight, Rachel could barely breathe. "Dennis," she gasped, and he loosened his grip.

"Sorry," he said meekly. "I got carried away."

Rachel couldn't help but smile. Dennis might be unthinking at times, but he was her man, and she loved him.

He leaned down and kissed her gently, then stepped back. "We, you, need to choose an engagement ring. Come with me," he said, and Rachel was perplexed. Where were they going?

"Our break is almost over," she protested, but Dennis pushed ahead anyway.

"I have a secret stash of rings in the safe," he told her. "I don't sell them often, but it's better than customers having to drive for an hour to buy a ring."

This revelation astonished Rachel. Holding her hand and pulling her along behind him, Dennis excitedly took her into the storeroom. The safe was hidden behind several boxes. Suddenly, she wished she didn't know where it was. What if someone came in for a ring and she was alone in the store? Still, it was better to be able to sell them if Dennis wasn't around. But what if they then tried to rob her?

She shook herself mentally. Her father was an enigma. He wasn't the norm, and she doubted Dennis's store would ever be robbed again. Surely one store couldn't be targeted more than once?

Rachel turned her back as he opened the safe—she didn't want to know the combination. Not yet anyway. Perhaps after they were married, it would be more appropriate.

"Oh, Dennis, they're beautiful," Rachel declared as she studied the dozen engagement rings on the tray. There was another tray still inside the safe, and her eyes strayed to those, too.

"They're wedding rings," he told her. "I've sold a lot of those over the past couple of years." He chuckled then. "You can choose one now, or later. Whatever you prefer."

Her eyes went back to the tray in his hands. "I can't choose. They are all magnificent."

His eyes lit up, and he grinned. "I chose them all myself. What about this one?" he said, taking one ring from the tray.

Rachel stared at it. "It looks very expensive. I'm sure you'd rather sell that one."

Dennis didn't answer immediately, but set the tray of remaining rings in the safe. He reached for her left hand and extended her finger. "Try it on, then decide." He slid the ring on and stared at it, but didn't offer an opinion.

"It's beautiful, Dennis. But I can't accept this ring— it is clearly worth a lot of money." Rachel adored it, but didn't want him to spend so much money on her.

"It's settled then," he said firmly. "This is the one." He reached out and held the ring on the sides. Rachel was of the opinion he was taking it to try another. Instead, he was checking for size. "It seems to fit perfectly. If you find it too tight, or too loose, let me know and we'll have it resized."

There was a knock at the door, and Dennis pulled out his pocket watch. "Time for the store to reopen. Would you mind? I need to lock up the safe again."

Mind? She'd love to. Rachel's heart and mind were in a whirl. She was getting married to the man of her dreams. Life couldn't get any better than that.

Faith stood on the other side of the door, little Elsie in her arms. Unlocking the door, Rachel wondered if Faith would notice the ring.

"Sorry, we lost track of time," she told her friend.

Faith studied her. "Really?" It was only one word, but it seemed to hold a lot of meaning.

"Can I help you with something?" Rachel said, using one of Dennis's favorite mantras with customers.

A sly smile crossed Faith's lips, then her eyes suddenly went to Rachel's hand. She squealed, startling both Rachel and Elsie. The baby cried, and Faith shushed her until she was calm again. "I came to see how you were feeling, but I can see there was no need." She raised her eyebrows. "Apparently, a lot can happen in the span of a morning." Faith leaned in and hugged Rachel. "Congratulations. When is the wedding?"

Dennis strolled out of the storeroom. "We haven't discussed that yet," he said. "Sooner than later, I think."

Rachel smiled. That suited her just fine.

It wasn't long before she was preparing to leave for the day when Sheriff Tommy Garrett arrived in the store.

"Good evening, Sheriff," Dennis said cordially. "What can I do to help you?"

The sheriff's expression was serious. "I've finally heard from the judge. He will be here the day after tomorrow, and you are both required to give evidence at the court case."

Rachel wasn't sure whether to be happy her ordeal would be finally over, or upset she needed to tell her story to a room full of strangers.

"There's something else," Tommy said, and Rachel had a feeling of foreboding. "Do you think you can come to the sheriff's office? I need to tell you something."

Rachel glanced at Dennis, and it was clear from his expression he had the same feelings overtake him. "My father is there," she said quietly. "Is there anywhere else we can talk?"

Dennis reached over and gently squeezed her hand. "I can lock up the store if you're happy to talk here," he said. "We can either go into the kitchen or the sitting room."

Tommy seemed to understand her apprehension about going to the sheriff's office. There was no privacy there, and her father would be in earshot. "The kitchen is fine," he said.

"I'll prepare coffee," Rachel said, and hurried ahead of them into the kitchen. Hopefully, her heart rate would slow by the time the men joined her.

She sat sipping tea by the time they came into the kitchen. What they'd been discussing without her, she didn't know, but she'd heard the murmur of voices. The moment Dennis came in, she knew the news was not good. He snatched up a mug of coffee and sat close beside her.

Sheriff Garrett sat down, then, seeming to choose his words carefully, spoke. "I'm not sure if this is good or bad news," he said, not taking his eyes from Rachel. Dennis's hand wrapped around hers. The movement wasn't lost on the sheriff. His eyes went to their entwined hands, then her engagement ring. A small smile tugged at his lips.

"It's about Bart Dougherty." The sheriff glanced at Dennis, who gave him the slightest of nods. Presumably, he already knew what Tommy was about to say. "He is not your father."

It took a moment for his words to sink in. Suddenly, a weight was lifted from Rachel's shoulders. "Praise the Lord," she said. Then the meaning of the sheriff's few words hit her. "If Bart is not my father…" She couldn't finish the sentence as reality set it.

"He murdered your real father when you were a small girl, stealing your real father's identity. He kidnapped both you and your mother."

Rachel was rocked to her core. "Who was my real father?" she asked, her voice unsteady. Rachel knew she was on the verge of breaking down. It meant Bart Dougherty had murdered both her parents. No wonder he didn't care for either Rachel or her mother.

"Bartholomew Dougherty was his name, and he was a highly respected preacher. It was our own preacher who set the investigation in motion. Apparently, you couldn't remember your so-called father when you were a small child."

"That's true. I couldn't recall him before I was about four or five." Tears rolled down her face, and Rachel wasn't sure if it was relief at knowing the man sitting in a jail cell wasn't her father, or if it was for a completely different reason. It was so very overwhelming.

"Who…who is the man who murdered my father?" Did she really want to know? It would all come out in the trial, anyway.

"Jeb McAllister, also known as *The Assassin*." The sheriff lifted his coffee for the first time and took a sip. "So named because he killed anyone who got in his way. Or if someone paid him to kill."

Rachel slumped backwards in her chair. Within moments, she felt Dennis's arm around her. How could anyone kill others with no thought for them? "That sounds like Bart. Um, Jeb. I've seen him murder at least a dozen men, and he didn't even flinch." She turned to the sheriff. "Thank you for telling me all this before the trial. It will give me time to absorb it all."

Sheriff Garrett stood then. Dennis kissed her cheek, then saw the sheriff out. He returned a short time later.

"It's a lot to take in," he said, his voice full of emotion. He pulled Rachel to her feet and enveloped her in his strong arms. Not for the first time, she was happy she landed in Crystal Springs and had gotten to know this wonderful man.

The man she would soon marry.

Chapter

Seventeen

Dennis had placed a sign on the door of the store the previous day, letting the townsfolk know the store would be closed. He didn't mention the court case, but everyone for miles around would be there, so there was no need.

He locked the front door, then went to the parsonage to collect Rachel. Both of them being star witnesses was nerve-wracking, but without them, there was no case. If it was the last thing he ever did, Dennis would ensure they jailed McAllister for the rest of his life at the least.

He knocked on the door, and Clyde answered. "Come in," he said. "Rachel won't be long. She's quite nervous about today." He ushered Dennis into the parlor. All he wanted to do was get to their destination, but for Rachel, he would do anything.

"I heard you were the one to realize the man on trial was not Rachel's father," Dennis said, trying to fill the silence. "Thank you. It's given her a lot of peace of mind. She never understood how her mother could marry a man like that."

"It was his name," Clyde said. "It seemed familiar. When I did some checking, he'd disappeared into obscurity, and no one had heard from him or his family again. I told the sheriff. He was the one who did all the hard work."

"Without you, none of this would have happened." Dennis was overcome with emotion. Until recently, he didn't really know the town preacher that well, but he now knew what a good man he really was. He was more than grateful for both Clyde and Faith caring for Rachel.

"Sorry to keep you waiting," Rachel said, standing in the doorway.

She was deathly pale, and it worried Dennis. He would keep a close eye on her today. Dennis couldn't protect her from the trial, but he could be there if she needed him. He stood and shook Clyde's hand. "Will you be there today?" he asked, praying that would be the case. Rachel may need his calming words. Clyde was good at what he did.

"I will." He turned to Rachel. "Reach out if you need me." He strolled to the door then and opened it. "May God bless you both, and keep you safe," he said as they left.

A shiver went down Dennis's spine. He wondered if they would need heavenly support. He certainly hoped not.

Dennis stood rigid on the witness stand. He didn't want to leave Rachel's side, but had no choice. Clyde moved forward and sat next to her as Dennis was called. It gave him the confidence to lay out the facts before the judge.

"Please state your name, address, and your relevance to this case," Judge Jonathan Harrigan said.

Dennis answered as clearly as he could.

"Now, Mr. Andrews, please explain what the accused did to you." He studied Dennis for mere seconds, then said, "We're all friends here. Provide as much information as you can."

Taking a long, fortifying breath, Dennis recalled the events of that terrible day. How he felt when the accused pushed a gun to his back, and how Rachel had run for help. He explained how she'd risked her own life to do so.

He was questioned about the effect it had on him, and although it went against the grain to disclose it, Dennis explained the anxiety that ensued.

He'd provided as much detail as possible, since the sheriff had briefed both himself and Rachel beforehand. Because of that, he knew it would build a case against Jeb McAllister.

"Thank you, Mr. Andrews. You may now step down."

His heart racing, Dennis returned to Rachel. She reached across and squeezed his hand, and it calmed him somewhat. It would be her turn next. Although it had been an ordeal for him, Dennis knew it would be far worse for Rachel.

"Miss Rachel Dougherty, please take the witness stand," Judge Harrigan said.

After she was sworn in, Rachel explained what the sheriff had told her about McAllister not being her father. There were mumbles throughout the room, and the judge slammed his gravel. "This is difficult for Miss Dougherty," he said firmly. "I demand quiet in my courtroom, or I will empty it except for witnesses."

Quiet ensued.

Rachel glanced across the room toward Jeb McAllister, a look of pure hate on her face. She told the judge of the murders she'd witnessed, most of which were mercantile owners. They'd been killed in the process of robberies. For no reason, except to ensure there were no witnesses. She'd watched him kill her mother to stop her talking.

It was then the room erupted.

"Shut yer mouth, yer stupid cow!" Jeb McAllister yelled as he endeavored to reach her. "I'll kill you. Yer know I will." It took both the sheriff and his deputy to restrain him from lunging at Rachel. Dennis was on his feet and by her side in mere seconds.

"Remove the prisoner," the judge demanded. "No, wait. I've heard enough," he said, then slammed his gavel again. Staring across the room, he declared, "Jeb McAllister, I find you guilty of fourteen counts of murder, one of attempted murder, and thirteen counts of robbery. The sentence is death by hanging."

As Dennis helped a relieved Rachel from the witness box, she fainted, and his heart was shattered. He hoped and prayed this would be the end of her ordeal.

"Someone fetch the doctor," the judge demanded, and Clyde obliged. Dennis stayed by Rachel's side until Marcus arrived, then moved aside.

He pulled smelling salts from his medical bag, and she quickly came around. "What happened?" Rachel asked as she stared up into Marcus's face.

"You fainted," Marcus told her, and ran his hands around her head.

"There are no bumps," Dennis told him. "I caught Rachel before she could hit the floor."

"And thank goodness you did," the doctor said, sounding relieved. Marcus offered his hand to Rachel, then helped her sit up. "We'll wait a few minutes before getting you to your feet."

Dennis watched as she glanced about. Was she searching for Jeb McAllister? "He's been taken back to the jail. He'll hang for his crimes." It was strange. Dennis thought the outcome would bring him a lot of peace. It didn't, and he wondered if it was the same for Rachel. She had endured so much because of the imposter who they now knew had murdered both her parents.

Marcus lifted Rachel's hand and checked her heart rate. "It's slowing down," he said, then clearly spotted the engagement ring. "This is new," he said, eyebrows raised as he glanced up at Dennis. "Congratulations to you both." He stood then and helped Rachel to her feet. "Shock is a funny thing," he said. "Even when the outcome is what we hope for, it can still affect us dearly." He handed Rachel off to Dennis. "You should feel better in a while. Take it easy for a few minutes."

"Thanks, Marcus," Dennis said. "I'll make sure she does."

Clyde stayed by their sides until Rachel was ready to leave. He didn't say a lot, but his calming presence was most welcome.

It wasn't long before everyone was ushered out of the room. The court was now closed, hopefully for a very long time to come.

#

#

The town was abuzz with talk of the upcoming nuptials. Faith and Clyde had rallied around Rachel, helping with the planning. Molly had all her lists ready and ensured everything would go smoothly.

With the trial behind them now, Rachel knew an enormous weight had been lifted from her shoulders. How she hadn't guessed that man, that murderer, wasn't her father, she would never know.

A knock on the door alerted her Dennis had arrived to take her to the sheriff's office. Jeb McAllister was to be hanged in two days. Today, though, he was being collected by marshals, and transported to Helena where he would be held until the hanging.

Rachel wanted to see for herself he was gone from Crystal Springs. She'd felt uneasy since he'd lunged at her in court, despite knowing he was locked behind bars. Dennis was by her side through it all. She couldn't believe how different he was with her, to the man portrayed by the townsfolk.

Arrogant, Dennis? She'd never seen it. The Dennis she knew was a loving and caring man. He had helped her when she needed it, and kept her safe when it was necessary. Most of all, he loved her.

And wasn't that really what mattered most?

They walked toward the sheriff's office in silence. Rachel stumbled at the site of the jail cart. Dennis quickly steadied her.

A team of four horses were ready and waiting, and a marshal stood near the back, ready to lock the prisoner up. Four more marshals came out of the jail, Jeb McAllister with them. He was chained, hands and feet—there was no way he was getting away.

Sheriff Garrett walked out with the marshals and stepped toward Rachel and Dennis. "Good riddance," Rachel said, bitterness clear in her voice.

"Two days and his life will be over," Tommy said.

"And ours will begin," Dennis said affectionately. "You are coming to the wedding, aren't you, Tommy?" he asked the sheriff.

"I didn't know I was invited."

"Everyone is invited. We'd love to see you there." Dennis pulled Rachel a little closer, and she didn't complain.

"Thank you for everything, Sheriff," Rachel said. "My heart is at peace now, knowing that monster is not my father. I wish I could bury both my parents, though," she said. "But that will never happen."

"I wasn't going to tell you yet, but McAllister reluctantly told us where to find their bodies. The marshals will endeavor to extricate their remains and bring them here."

Rachel's heart exploded. All she needed now was to marry the man she loved. She wasn't sure she could wait two more days, but knew there was little choice.

Molly and Faith stood at the entrance to the church with Rachel, and ensured her gown sat perfectly. Faith handed her a bouquet of beautiful flowers. Most of them from the store, the rest from Faith's garden.

Rachel had admired that garden from the moment she stepped foot on the property. She brought the bouquet to her face and breathed in their enticing fragrance.

"I think you're ready," Faith whispered, then the two women scurried to the front of the church. Her heart pounding, Rachel stepped inside and glanced about. Her two best friends had decorated the church beautifully with ribbons Dennis had supplied. It amazed her how much the people of Crystal Springs had been willing to do for her. Especially after everything that happened.

The organ music played, and Rachel took a tentative step forward. Then another, and another, her eyes on her groom-to-be. Until today, she'd never seen Dennis look so handsome. She'd seen him in a suit at church, but this was new. He'd kept it a secret, one she was happy for him to keep.

She glanced down at the beautifully made beige gown she wore. Alice Goldie really was as good a dressmaker as everyone said.

Clyde stood at the altar, his well-used Bible open, ready for the ceremony. This town had opened their hearts and their homes to her, and Rachel knew she could never repay them. Taking her last few steps toward Dennis, she wondered how she had been so lucky. Although Dennis told Rachel it was he who had been the winner in this arrangement.

Rachel took her place next to Dennis at the altar, and Clyde's nod was almost indecipherable. The ceremony was about to begin. "Dearly beloved," he said, and Rachel's heart was filled with joy. Never in her life did she believe marriage was in her future. Living on the run with a gunslinger was not the life she'd envisioned, but now she knew love was everything, and she had a long and happy life to look forward to with Dennis Andrews, the town's former matchmaker.

Almost a month later, Rachel stood in the tiny cemetery not far from Crystal Springs, Dennis by her side. It was an unusually bleak day, but the townsfolk had come out to support her despite the unwelcoming weather.

She glanced down at the two graves sitting side by side, their engraved headstones already in place. A firm arm snaked around her waist, and Rachel knew Dennis was there to support her. It hadn't been easy, but the authorities had found her parents' bodies from the sketchy information provided by Jeb McAlister. The man who she had believed to be her father for most of her life. The man who, unbeknownst to Rachel, had murdered her real father and taken her family hostage. All to make it easier to rob stores.

Rachel glanced up at Dennis. "I still can't believe he murdered my family for greed." A tear escaped from her eye, but Rachel didn't try to hold back this time. She knew finally having her parents together again was the last thing she could do for them as her daughter.

Suddenly, the preacher's voice cut through her thoughts. "Today is a day for rejoicing," Clyde said, then studied Rachel. "For many years, Preacher Bartholomew Dougherty was missing, along with his family. Today they are reunited."

She knew his words to be true, but it didn't stop her tears from falling. Dennis pulled her closer still and held her tight. Clyde continued with his kind and gentle words, and Rachel felt comforted. With her parents reunited, she could now find peace.

After the official ceremony was over, Rachel stood in the deserted cemetery. She'd told Dennis she wanted time alone with her parents, without everyone from town. Thankfully, he'd understood.

"Mama, Papa," she said, tears in her eyes. She glanced up at him, and Dennis put a loving arm around her. "I truly wish you were both here to meet my wonderful husband, and to one day see our babies grow up. I love you both so much." The tears flowed, and Rachel knew she would often visit her parent's graves. She also knew Dennis would support her in that endeavor.

 Epilogue

Two years later…

Rachel sat quietly in Faith and Clyde's parlor. Elsie was running around and urging little Bartholomew to run with her. "He can't run, Elsie," Faith told her almost three-year-old daughter. "He's still learning to walk."

Sudden crying alerted Rachel that Clyde and Faith's six-month-old baby was awake. "I'll get him up," Clyde said, a smile on his face.

There was no mistaking the pride he felt. Dennis knew exactly how his friend was feeling. He was no longer a bitter and arrogant man, but through love and guidance, he had become the person he knew he should always have been.

He studied his beautiful wife, sitting opposite him. She was glowing, and he had no doubt she was as happy with her life as Dennis was with his. Instead of being known as the arrogant storekeeper, he was now friends with many of the townsfolk. They attended church functions as a family, and Rachel, although she'd never forgotten her ordeal, continued to look to the future.

Dennis shoved his hand in his pocket and pulled out a small paper bag. "Candy!" Elsie shouted, her little eyes wide with excitement. "May I, Mama?" she asked, her little voice almost pleading.

Although he knew he shouldn't, Dennis always brought candy for Elsie. It was an unwritten agreement between him and the Walters that every time they visited, candy would be an accompaniment. He could barely contain his grin.

"You're such a softie," Faith told Dennis. He knew he was. "Of course you can have candy, Elsie," she told her daughter. "Uncle Dennis really does spoil you." It was Faith's turn to smile, and it warmed Dennis's heart.

It wasn't lost on him that two years earlier, he would have frowned on this very thing. Little did he know how much he was missing with his gruff ways. Looking back, he realized how truly unhappy he'd been. Everything changed the day he met Rachel. The same day he was certain he would die.

As if she could read his mind, Rachel began to stand. Dennis was quickly on his feet, his hands wrapped around her. "Thank you," Rachel said. "It's getting more difficult to stand up these days."

Dennis didn't doubt it. With only a few weeks to go before baby number two arrived, getting around had become difficult for his wife.

"Are you sure you don't mind us leaving Bartholomew here?" Rachel quizzed Faith, not for the first time.

"Of course not. Elsie loves having him over to play. Take your time. I know it's difficult for you." Faith stood as Clyde entered the room, her arms outreached for her young son.

When he checked, little Bartholomew was busy playing and didn't notice they were leaving. The pair quietly left, but would return soon from Rachel's check up with the doctor.

Dennis loved Rachel more than life itself, and didn't know how he'd survived without her. His wife, and their little son, meant to the world to him.

Family was the most important thing in the entire world to Dennis now. Rachel had taught him far more than living life to the full outside of his business. She'd taught him love was everything. It was a lesson he would never forget.

He silently said a prayer of thanks for everything God had blessed him with, especially his growing family.

From the Author

Thank you so much for reading my book – I hope you enjoyed it.

I would greatly appreciate you leaving a review where you purchased, even if it is only a one-liner. It helps to have my books more visible!

~*~

Multi-published, award-winning and bestselling author Cheryl Wright, former secretary, debt collector, account manager, writing coach, and shopping tour hostess, loves reading.

She writes both historical and contemporary western romance, as well as romantic suspense.

She lives in Melbourne, Australia, and is married with two adult children and has six grandchildren. When she's not writing, she can be found in her craft room making greeting cards.

Website: *http://www.cheryl-wright.com/*

Facebook Reader Group:
https://www.facebook.com/groups/cherylwrightaut hor/

Join My Newsletter:

https://cheryl-wright.com/newsletter/
(and receive a free book)

www.ingramcontent.com/pod-product-compliance
Lightning Source LLC
Chambersburg PA
CBHW072147130726
47909CB00004BB/1250